IN BUFFALO WITH YOU

IN BUFFALO WITH YOU

MEGAN FUENTES

In Buffalo With You Copyright © by Megan Fuentes. All Rights Reserved.

To anyone who has ever needed to believe in themselves a little harder.

Contents

Chapter One
Tommy 1

Chapter Two
Linda 7

Chapter Three
Tommy 15

Chapter Four
Linda 23

Chapter Five
Tommy 29

Chapter Six
Linda 35

Chapter Seven
Tommy 41

Chapter Eight
Linda 47

Chapter Nine
Tommy 51

Chapter Ten
Linda 57

Chapter Eleven 63
Chapter Twelve 69
Your Reader Treats 75
IN CHARLESTON WITH YOU: Chapter One
Jacob 77
IN CHARLESTON WITH YOU: Chapter Two
Genevieve 85

About the Author 93

CHAPTER ONE

Tommy

In Tommy's view, the best thing—indeed, one of the few undeniably good things—about being a young newspaper hawker at the turn of the century was the sunrises. He relished the slap of feet on the pavement and the night's cool air melting into daytime warmth, but nothing beat a cloudless, radiant sunrise like the one he'd witness peeking over Buffalo's skyline within the hour.

Everywhere he went, he could count on a pretty sunrise to start his morning, just as he could count on the morning parade of newsies. Tommy could always tell when there were new kids joining him on the sidewalk. The newer you were to the job, the more you craned your neck as you walked up the sleeping streets to buy your bundle of newspapers. The new kids walked slower, too, oblivious to the favoritism shown to the earliest newsies, who snapped up all the papers without egregious ink smudges and bent corners.

Tommy knew better, but he didn't act like it. He cast his eyes skyward as often as any of them. Before dawn, the pinpricks of starlight in the lightening sky soothed him with the promises of a new day, and a chance for things to improve.

Until someone inevitably tried to run him over.

The smack to the middle of Tommy's back stole his breath, and he almost stumbled forward as he hissed a string of expletives.

"Oh, so sorry about that, mister, so sorry!"

The high pitch of the voice alone would've given him pause,

but "mister?" Tommy turned around to find that the newsie who'd shoved him was two-thirds his height and perhaps half his age—about ten or so.

Before Tommy could reassure the boy there was no harm done, one of the other, more experienced newsies hollered at him from up the street. "Hey, what happened to those quick feet of yours, Tommy Rabbit?"

Without missing a beat, Tommy flashed a winning smile at his peer and kicked up his feet in the air, which got him and half a dozen of the other boys laughing.

"Wow," whispered the boy. "How'd you learn to jump like that? Are you really Tommy Rabbit, from the paper? Could you teach me that?"

Tommy rubbed the back of his neck. The kid must've been staring at that article for hours to be able to make out his tiny, grainy face in the background of that picture with Kid Blink and the rest. They'd all appeared side by side in an article after the news broke that the strike had reached as far as Providence, Rhode Island. Weeks later, after the union had more or less fallen to pieces, Tommy was trekking northeast, selling whatever paper the town he planned to sleep in that night had to offer.

The strike's success in rallying the troops had amazed Tommy. He wasn't very high up in their little makeshift union's ranks two years ago—though he was one of their oldest at eighteen—but he was good enough friends to get an earful whenever he wanted. And there was always lots to hear about.

Then a deal was struck, and the fire they'd stoked over two hard-fought weeks died out overnight. The union disbanded, and everyone went their separate ways.

Tommy pushed back the brim of the boy's frayed tweed cap to get a better look at him in the dim morning light. "I need to know your name before I give away all my trade secrets."

The boy's face twisted up in thought, then: "Cappie McCoy."

It wasn't that the boy had so clearly nicknamed himself just that second that got Tommy chuckling, and it wasn't the way "Cappie" took a bow so deep, the cap came off altogether. It was a combination of the two, plus a recognizable gleam in his eye. "How about you try that again, 'Cappie?'"

The boy kicked a rock in his path. "Well, that's what I'd sure like to be called. But my real name is Clancy McCoy."

"Well, I can appreciate the pluck, but you don't go nicknaming yourself. Where's the fun in that? You gotta earn your nickname."

Clancy mulled this over as the pair began walking again. "So how did all creation come to call you Tommy Rabbit?"

Tommy knew the question was coming, but that didn't prevent his heart from leaping into his throat. And if he told Clancy the truth, he knew which questions would come next—how he could possibly eke out a living on the pennies he earned per day, how he came to Buffalo, whether he planned to stay in this city, this time, at least a little while.

The answers would only disappoint poor Clancy. And any explanation Tommy could offer could only make him feel worse.

Tommy considered making something up, but that was no use. If Clancy was anything like the other young newsboys that'd taken a shine to him, he'd sniff out the truth in a second. It was one thing to lie and get away with it, but it was worse to be caught in the lie, then have to wriggle your way out of it.

"*Well?*"

Clancy's insistence startled him. They must've been walking in silence for a while. Tommy cleared his throat. "I'd like to save that story for another time, if it's all the same to you. Besides"—he gestured with an open palm—"we're here already."

Across the street, the sun was not quite peeking over the top of the building that housed the *Buffalo Express*. It was a usual-looking building. Only the hand-painted letters on the awning betrayed its identity, but that was more than a big enough clue for newsies, who'd already formed a line outside the door, two blocks long.

Most of the kids were on the younger side. Their eyes weren't on the twinkling stars or the rising sun anymore, but on their little hands that held their coins. Some picked them up, turned them over, then put them back down again. Some cupped both hands like they'd trapped a firefly. They did this while chatting with their peers, debating what the clouds were trying to tell them about the day's weather.

Tommy frowned at the sight. *See, this is why the union shouldn't've given up so easily,* he thought. He cast a glance at Clancy, who had dug out his own money to count and recount.

Clancy must've felt the eyes on him, because he looked up at Tommy and said, "What?"

"I was just wondering what you're doing here, that's all."

Clancy's brow furrowed. "My old man was in the army, and he hasn't come home, so Mom had me read the *Express* and the *Courier* and a lot of other newspapers to decide which one I liked the best to sell. I picked the *Express*." He beamed. "And I'm glad I did because I got to meet you, Tommy Rabbit! You're living history, you know that?"

The door to the *Buffalo Express* swung open. Tommy couldn't tell much else about what was going on from where he stood, but suddenly the line began to shrink instead of grow, and all the newsies came to life as whispers of what the day's headlines shot up and down the line.

Tommy knew you couldn't trust half of them, but one rumor about the day's news in particular interested him. He didn't let himself get caught up in the excitement until he and Clancy were inside the building, four kids away from where a portly man the other newsies called Mr. Langhorne distributed the bundles. Only then, when he caught a glimpse of the words printed in black and white, did Tommy believe it.

M'KINLEY WILL DO THE PAN!

It could be exactly what he'd been wishing on all those stars for.

"What are you smiling for?" Mr. Langhorne huffed.

Tommy just shook his head as he slid the dimes across the wooden counter. With a wink in Clancy's direction, he slid two fingers under the twine that held the papers together and used his other hand to beckon Clancy to follow him, ignoring the wide eyes of the other newsies.

"But I haven't—"

"Don't worry about it," Tommy said, winking again.

Tommy led them out of the *Buffalo Express* and down Washington Street. When he was sure the other newsies were out of earshot and wouldn't get overexcited, he gestured to the headline.

"I don't get it," Clancy said.

"Can't you read, li'l McCoy? The President of these United States is coming to Buffalo to see the Pan-American Exposition. And he's coming in a week!"

Clancy shrugged.

"Let me paint you a picture." Tommy slipped the top paper out of the stack, shoved the paper into Clancy's hands, and threw his arm around Clancy's shoulder. "President McKinley arrives at the Pan. He meets with the people. He shakes hands with the people. Maybe he shakes my hand, huh? Maybe I can bend his ear for a minute?"

"And tell him what?"

"And tell him about this kid I know named Clancy McCoy—"

"Cappie McCoy!"

Tommy chuckled. "Right, sure, *Cappie*. And I tell him about the plights of all the little newsboys and newsgirls—and our brothers and sisters who work in factories, canneries, farms, and mines. We're paid less than grown-ups for work that's just as or more dangerous. And why, 'cause we're shorter? 'Cause we're told to listen to adults who know so much more?" Tommy shook his head. "That's not right. We're lucky to sell papers, no mistake about it, but not because we get to drop out of school and be *entrepreneurs*—because so many other kids have it worse. You ever seen a kid your age with a limp, or with part of their hand missing?"

"Sure, loads of times."

"Well, how d'you think that happened?"

Clancy paled, which was exactly the kind of response Tommy was hoping to get from McKinley.

This was it. Tommy could feel it. *The* chance to make things better for the newsies.

Clancy glanced at the bundle of papers. "Is that why you bought so many?"

Tommy nodded. "I took a gamble. This is triple what I usually buy. How much did your mom give you to buy papers this morning?"

Clancy brought out his coins again, and Tommy watched him mouth the numbers to himself. "Thirty."

Tommy loosened the twine around his newspapers, ran his finger down the stack, and pulled out fifty. "Take these and keep your money, all right? Maybe this'll give you a good head start, so you don't have to come back so many times. But until then, how'd you like to be a team? We'll sell your fifty papers first and get you your money for your family, and then we can work on selling the rest of mine. As a duo. What do you say?"

Clancy's grin was so wide, Tommy thought the boy's teeth might pop right right out. Then the light in his eyes faded. "What about your family?"

"I don't have one, and that serves me well here. I don't have to take money home at all—I'll save it all. I don't care if I have to skip my coffee and ration a bagel to last me the whole day." Tommy placed his hand on top of Clancy's cap like he imagined McKinley would've placed his hand on the Bible as he was sworn into office, with his other hand raised high in the air. "Clancy, I swear to you on my honor that I'm going to purchase myself a ticket to the Pan-American Exposition, I'm going to meet President McKinley, and you're going to see the whole world turned on its head. Just you wait."

CHAPTER TWO

Linda

The new typewriter ribbon finally in place, Linda allowed herself a glance out the window. The sun was just beginning its descent, and—as if only now realizing the time—the bell signaling the end of the working day rang out.

Just my luck. Typing up the rest of her boss's notes would have to wait until the following day. There would be no staying late to finish, either; Aggie was already out of her chair and striding towards her.

Linda winced as Aggie perched herself on the edge of the desk, hoping the rest of the office floor wasn't looking their way. "Well, you ran over here like greased lightning, didn't you?"

Aggie tucked a few blonde strands of hair back into place, obviously guiltless. "That's because I want to go home. I don't suspect that's any big secret to the folks around here." Aggie frowned. "I didn't finish those last couple of chapters of *The Wonderful Wizard of Oz*, so I'm afraid I'll make for a dull companion on the walk home."

Her things packed, Linda stood and walked with Aggie to the stairs. "That's fine, Aggie. I did. Do you want me to tell you what happens?"

"Good heavens, yes! You tell it better anyway. And don't play modest—you know you do."

Linda waved away the compliment, but truth be told, she knew she had something of a knack for stories. It was a talent picked up from many years of playing governess to her younger siblings.

She had six of them total, all of them three years her junior or greater—Angelina, Charles, Joseph, Nina, David, and Dante.

One might expect Angelina, her closest in age at fifteen, to be her favorite, but it was Nina who owned Linda's heart. They were each other's favorite audience by leagues—Nina enjoyed Linda's stories, and Linda loved watching Nina perform. Such a talent she had! Her voice was as clear and sweet as any songbird. She was the spitting image of Linda at that age, too, which might have helped endear Nina to her—round cheeks, a small mouth, and long, thick curly hair that telegraphed to the world their Italian heritage.

Their father would be picking Nina up from the Pan-American Exposition later in the evening, after Nina had exhausted herself singing aboard a gondola in the Midway for visitors. At the Pan, they called her Baby Patti, and people tossed pennies when they stopped to watch. Papà promised the whole family would do the Pan soon, and Linda couldn't stand the wait to watch the youngest Morgana daughter dazzle onlookers. At the end of the night, Nina would come back barely able to keep her eyes open, but willing to cuddle up close with the rest of her siblings as Linda read aloud a story.

If only this arrangement could be kept forever.

Stepping out onto the sidewalk along with the rest of the office worker bees, Linda and Aggie surveyed the street corners, searching for their respective little brothers. Normally, all three boys could be found just across the way, their expressions dependent on how many papers they they sold, their pockets jingling with coins.

But they weren't in their usual places. A lump formed in Linda's throat, and it grew larger with every passing second until Aggie nudged her with an elbow.

"What is it? Do you see them?"

Aggie nodded to a spot two blocks down. "Isn't that them all the way over there?"

Linda's relief was short-lived. There they were, sweaty and

smiling, listening to someone. His back was to her, but what little she could see of him only sprouted new questions in her mind. The stranger was dressed all casually, like he was one of the newsboys—no coat, just a button-down and trousers with a well-worn cap on his short, dark hair—but he looked just a hair too old. And he was sticking around too long to be an ordinary customer.

As she watched his animated gesticulations, Linda's imagination ran wild. What was he doing? Trying to sell them snake oil? Recruit them? Or was he some crazed drifter who could show how batty he really was at any second?

Linda turned to Aggie. "Do you know who that is with them?"

Aggie shook her head.

Linda stayed quiet as they marched over, sidestepping all the men in suits and their female assistants. If they were lucky, they might catch a word or two of what he was saying, and they'd know how concerned they should be.

Unfortunately, Linda failed to communicate this before Aggie executed her own strategy. With apparently no regard at all for how uncouth she might look, she cupped her hands around her mouth and shouted, "Clarence Albert McCoy!"

The stranger turned around as if his name had been called, and for a moment, Linda forgot she was supposed to be wary of him. However disheveled his appearance, his features were quite handsome. His jawline was strong, his eyes playful, and the pink in his cheeks from the September sun gave him a cheeriness that matched the easy smile he wore.

More magnetic than what he actually looked like was the air about him. An energy radiated from him, like the electricity in the air before lightning struck. He was out of breath, too. Whatever he'd been discussing with the boys must have been exhilarating. She wanted to know what he was saying.

Then Linda's good sense returned to her, and she was all the more suspicious. Of all people, the charming ones were the most dangerous. She should know that by now.

The stranger spoke with a warm and husky voice so thickly accented, he could have only come from Manhattan. "Clancy 'Cappie' McCoy is your baby brother? He and his friends here are fine newsies. You ought to be proud."

"I am, thank you." Aggie wiped a bit of dirt from Clancy's trousers, hardly looking at the stranger. "But we have to be going now."

He should have been talking to Aggie, since it was she who Clancy sauntered towards, but his eyes were on Linda. "Oh, are you sure?"

Linda looked down to avoid meeting his gaze. "Yes, we're afraid so. David, Dante, come along. Our parents are waiting for us."

Dante, the baby of the family at just seven years old, stuck out his bottom lip. It was a move that would've worked miracles on their mother, but to which Linda was immune. David pouted, too, and whined, "But Tommy was just going to tell us about how he helped turn over a wagon!"

"Hey, hey," Tommy said, hands up in front of him, as if he expected an attack. "I wasn't *advocatin'* for it. I was just relaying the facts of the matter." When Aggie and Linda only glared back, he straightened his cap. "I can finish the story tomorrow, Davey."

Linda ushered for Aggie and the boys to start walking towards home. "Oh, no, you can't, actually. Our brothers only sell papers on Mondays and Tuesdays. They'll be in school for the rest of the week."

"But I'll see you tomorrow, won't I?" He nodded towards the door of the *Buffalo Express*. "You and Miss McCoy work upstairs. The boys told me. And little Dante was telling me how their oldest sister Linda never turned down telling them a bedtime story if they asked nicely. That's you, ain't it? Would you be so kind as to pass along my stories?"

Like hell.

That's what Linda wanted to say—perhaps even what she *should've* said—but all she could muster were some mumblings about her mother having supper ready soon. She turned and started up the street, walking as quickly as she could without appearing to rush. Aggie slowed to meet her, and the boys walked five feet ahead, out of earshot, mimicking their new older friend's accent as they talked about their day.

Linda tucked an errant curl behind her ear, ignoring Aggie's eyebrow raise. "So, Glinda the Good Witch—"

"You're woefully mistaken if you think I'm going to let you avoid talking about what I just witnessed between you and that man."

"I'm sure I don't know what you mean. Oh, drat! Boys," Linda called out, "where did you leave your unsold papers? If we hurry back, Mr. Langhorne might still be in his office and buy them back!"

Casual as anything, David replied over his shoulder, "We sold them all."

Linda and Aggie exchanged looks. Sold them all? That couldn't be right. They'd never pulled that off before, not one of them. And it wasn't like the headlines were thrilling.

Clancy turned around and flashed his grin, missing front teeth and all. "Tommy Rabbit taught us how to sell papers! He's the smartest newsie *ever*."

The stranger. Linda shook her head. What kind of a name was Tommy Rabbit? She'd heard the newsboys—especially the ones who were on the run—often went by nicknames, but Tommy Rabbit just seemed silly. And just what sort of strategies did Mr. Rabbit see fit to teach her and Aggie's impressionable young siblings?

"*Linda*," Aggie said in a tone that suggested it was far from the first time Aggie tried to get her attention.

Linda winced. "Ah, yes. So, in the penultimate chapter of *The Wonderful Wizard of Oz*—"

"Stop that. You found him nice-looking, didn't you?"

Cheeks aflame, Linda knew she was caught. "This isn't proper to discuss in front of our brothers, let alone on the streets, where other people can hear our private business—"

"It also isn't *proper* to be walking through town without a chaperone. Or to have a vocation. *Or*—well, you understand what I mean."

Aggie had cut herself off, but Linda knew what she was going to say next. It was unthinkable that two young ladies such as themselves should be nearing twenty and lacking prospects for husbands.

Aggie liked the idea of being a devil-may-care spinster, but Linda's circumstances were wholly different. Aggie's mother had only her and Clancy to look after, so it didn't matter so much if she stayed at home for a little longer than normal. Linda's parents, on the other hand, had more than half a dozen mouths to feed, and no engagement for any of them on the horizon.

Well, Linda *was* engaged once. But he was long gone now. She'd cried those tears, and now she was focused on the important things in life—helping her family.

And Tommy Rabbit—who, in a single day, taught her little brothers how to grift and beg and all sorts of other new ways to cause trouble, she was sure—was bound to cause her headaches. With any luck, he'd skip town or find a new paper to work for or in some other way disappear before she'd be forced to see him again. Before her brothers could see him again.

"Aggie, I can't imagine what you think you saw taking place, but rest assured that I won't be accepting any calling card of his anytime soon."

Frowning, Aggie picked up Linda's hand and gave it a pat. "Perhaps I was mistaken. I don't think so, but I'll admit that in my long history of conversing with you, I've been wrong once or twice before." She narrowed her eyes. "I suppose I *could* be wrong again."

"If you'd prefer to discuss how wrong or right you've been since the dawn of our friendship to hearing what becomes of Scarecrow—"

"Oh, curse you, Linda Berenice Morgana! You know he's my favorite!"

Linda gave Aggie a mischievous grin, then began her synopsis, happy to allow disquieting thoughts of that Tommy Rabbit character to float out of her head.

For now.

CHAPTER THREE

Tommy

The alliance with Clancy McCoy and the Morgana brothers was Tommy's best idea yet. Thanks to his new young friends' cherubic faces and his advertising skills, he'd had the money to pay for a week's rent at a lodging house before the day was through.

Well, he had the money, but he didn't use it. Instead, he spent an unseasonably chilly night sleeping on the back stoop of a tenement house with a few other newsies, using day-old newspapers for bedding.

It was not the hardest night Tommy had spent on the streets of the Empire State, but it wasn't the most pleasant by any stretch. The same vermin he'd encountered in Manhattan, Syracuse, and Rochester had followed him here, too, and they took turns disrupting his light sleep all through the night. But whenever a rat scurried across the wood, or a spider crawled over his pant leg, Tommy pictured himself at the Pan-American Exposition, shaking President McKinley's hand. As uncomfortable as he might've been in the moment, he would be a thousand times more upset if he wasn't permitted to come within a hundred yards of the President because he wasn't washed up and dressed in his Sunday best. No, he needed to save every penny for his appearance at the Pan.

Tommy returned to the *Buffalo Express* the following morning and found no Clancy, Davey, or Dante among the morning parade, just as Linda Morgana had said. In a way, he didn't mind that there were fewer newsies running about. The less competition, the easier it would be to earn the money he needed. But he would miss the boys' company. In just that single day, they'd grown on him, and he was intent on teaching them more about being a good newsie and earning money in honest ways.

That is, if the McCoy and Morgana gals would let him.

What rotten luck that they worked for the paper. He couldn't be sure what kind of talk went on upstairs about the newsies who came to buy papers with dirty shirts and holes in their trousers, but he didn't imagine the pictures they painted were flattering. What must they think of him?

What must Miss Morgana think of him?

No, he knew. She thought of him as a bad egg. She didn't care beans about him.

Too bad he couldn't say the feeling was mutual. Linda Morgana had interested him immediately. Never mind her beauty—though the richness of the black in her hair and the brown in her eyes was striking, and the image of her skirt gliding as she walked away was in his head for the rest of the evening—because anyone could be beautiful. Only she could have such a fearsome, bewitching presence. Davey and Dante fell right in line when she showed up. From the way they spoke about her that afternoon, she was the steadiest thing they had in their lives. There was always a story at night when you requested it, a kind word when you wanted it, and a stern talking-to when you needed it.

That surety was exactly why he hadn't approached her when he saw her walking home again alongside Miss McCoy. She'd made it clear that she wanted nothing to do with him, and he didn't want to catch her wrath, nor cause her any discomfort.

To distract himself from the urge to talk to her, Tommy sold papers. Every day, he bought twenty more than he had the previous day. And every day, Mr. Langhorne would peer over his spectacles, grunt, and hand over the goods.

In Barcelona With You

"I'm starting to think you're eating them, boy," Mr. Langhorne said the day before Tommy was meant to do the Pan.

"He ain't eating them, Mister," one newsie said in his defense. "Which is unfortunate. If he were, I'd be going home with a few more pennies in my pocket tonight."

Tommy grinned apologetically in reply. He'd been particularly ruthless in his pursuit of customers, and being so new in town, he didn't blend into the background like the newsies who called Buffalo their home. He was different, and he knew how to get a passerby's attention. Selling papers in New York City helped him hone his instincts for knowing exactly the right way to word a headline for the working man, the woman with a babe on her hip, and the high society types.

Those advantages, plus a little luck and every cent of his savings, and Tommy found himself handing over his ticket to enter the Pan-American Exposition on the morning of September the sixth, 1901, through the Elmwood Gate.

Miraculously, he'd made it.

Pride swelled in his chest, and his eyes were the widest they'd ever been, straining to take in all that the exposition had to offer as the crowd demanded he keep a steady pace. Like a fish trapped in a current, Tommy was being pushed and pulled by the masses past the lush gardens and the electric fountain on his right. Everyone headed towards the behemoth that was neatly labeled on his map to be the Electric Tower.

When he closed his eyes last night, Tommy pictured stately marble buildings with pillars and columns, as though imported from Greece or Rome. Instead, the exposition was awash with vibrant color—rich reds, blues, greens, and golds of every shade coated architecture that seemed to him like castles.

He'd seen pictures of the expositions of yesteryears the few times he'd snuck into libraries at night, when cold weather prohibited sleeping outside. He thought them magnificent even captured as they were in black and white photographs viewable only by the dim candle light, but seeing them live and vivid before him was more spectacular than he would've dared dream.

He wished the other newsies—*all* the other newsies—could see it before it became yesterday's news.

That desire gave way to memories of Davey, Dante, and Clancy. Then, for the thousandth time since meeting her, Miss Linda Morgana danced into his mind. He shook his head as if to dislodge the picture. It was probably best to forget about her. To forget about her brothers, and probably Clancy and Miss McCoy, too. But he was no good at getting his train of thought to stay on the schedule he set.

Remember why you're here, he told himself. *You're here on behalf of newsies everywhere. The kiddos who have no one else to stick up for 'em. You're going to meet McKinley and—real politely—demand he do better for them.*

But rumor had it that McKinley wouldn't be addressing the public until later in the day, so he had at least a few hours on his hands. At the moment, Tommy had a hankering for a cup of coffee despite the heat. He circled the southwestern portion of the Pan, looking for some small kiosk to take his dime. He found none. Just as he was preparing himself to settle for soda water, the whole left side of his body took a wallop that knocked him to the ground, his brand new derby hat flying off his head and into the shrubbery that lined the walkways.

The first part of him to recover from the assault was his mouth. "Jeez, doesn't anyone in this town know how to walk?"

"Oh, I'm sorry, I was—oh!"

He recognized the voice—dulcet in tone, with the slightest hint of an Italian accent. He rolled over and sat up straight to see who was sprawled out on the ground beside him. Sure enough, Tommy found himself looking into the soulful brown eyes he'd thought of scores of times since his first encounter with them. "Miss Morgana?"

She blinked at him, then recoiled. "Is that you, Mr. Rabbit?"

Tommy stood, stifling chuckles all the way up. "I'm Mr. Reid, actually." He clapped his hands together to get the dirt off and offered his hand.

Whether her cheeks were rosy from the sun, the embarrassment of having run into him, or something else, Tommy couldn't say for sure, but he liked to think the blush was for him. "You look so different," she said as she accepted the help rising to her feet.

"I wanted to look a huckleberry above my persimmon." Tommy retrieved his hat from the bush and placed it on his head, gesturing to his whole body once his outfit was once again complete. "How'd I do?"

Whatever she was going to stay died before it left her mouth, killed by something horrific over Tommy's shoulder. He turned around and picked out a lone, unshaven man with a brown fedora among a sea of people. The man was alone, but he scanned the crowds as if looking for someone. He didn't seem to be panicked; he wasn't missing someone from his party. He was leaning forward, his muscles tensed and ready to pounce—looking for prey.

Tommy had passed many of his kind on the streets of New York City. He'd watched them stare after women—or girls, or other men, or boys—from the opposite street corner, like a cat stalking a mouse. Tommy was immediately reminded of a time just before the newsies strike was underway, when a girl newsie asked him and a few of his friends to walk her back to the lodging house because someone with the same perverted hunger in his eyes had followed her for six blocks.

The man with the brown fedora set his eyes at last on Linda.

Then he saw Tommy standing beside her, and his posture changed. The shoulders relaxed, and he chiseled a tight smile onto his features as he closed the distance between them. As he approached, the sour stench of beer strengthened until its effects were nigh-overpowering. His words blended into one another as he said, "Thank you, sir, for finding my fiancée."

"I am *not*—"

Linda's sentence was cut off by her own yelp as the man reached out and grabbed her by the upper arm. As if her denial wasn't a fine enough reason to believe the man was lying, the utter lack of affection in the way the man dug his fleshy fingers into her blouse was plenty of evidence for Tommy. Then, when she tried to use her other arm to reach up—to grab her hatpin and defend herself, perhaps—he wrapped his arm all the way around her shoulders, squeezing her tight, rendering movement impossible.

"Forgive her," the man growled. "She's been hysterical since we got here. I think it's time we went home."

Tommy's mind raced. He had to help Linda, but he also couldn't draw too much attention or have it come to blows. If he caused enough hullabaloo to land him in trouble with the authorities, he'd never get the chance to talk to McKinley. "You say this is your fiancée?"

"Yeah."

"That's funny. I think you must have the wrong lady. I didn't see you at supper last week."

The man squinted. "What do you mean?"

"Well, she's my fiancée, too."

Tommy reached out for her, and Linda's eyes widened. Her breathing was heavy, and he could see from her darting eyes and pursed lips that she was desperately trying to think of any other way out of her situation. Tommy stretched out his fingers and curled them insistently. *Just grab my hand, Miss Morgana. I can be your way out. Trust me, please.*

She gave Tommy a once-over that lasted for a hundred years. Then, slowly, Linda slipped her hand into his, and the man released his iron grip.

Tommy shivered as relief flooded his body like a drug. Wrapping her hand around his forearm, he spoke quickly to leave no room for argument. "Ain't she the most beautiful girl in the world? Ain't I lucky? Ain't you lucky you got to meet her? Thanks for reuniting us. Shame we've got to skidoo now. I hope you find *your* fiancée. I'm sure she's around here somewhere."

Tommy turned himself and Linda around to hurry towards the center of the fair. If the man in the brown fedora decided to follow them, he'd have to search high and low to catch sight of them among the masses as they made their way in a zigzag fashion.

When they arrived at the Court of the Fountains—with the almighty Electric Tower's 16-foot gilded goddess of light smiling down upon them, and the four main pavilions standing sentry on both sides—Linda's trance state was broken. She squirmed out of Tommy's light hold and spun in a slow circle, difficult as that was with hordes of people surrounding them.

"It's a lot to take in, I know."

She nodded, but instead of marveling at the wonders of man's ingenuity as the architects intended, Linda's mouth dropped open in horror.

Tommy frowned. Did panic ever leave her eyes?

"Are you all right, Miss Morgana?"

"No, Mr. Reid," she said, trembling. "I am utterly lost."

CHAPTER FOUR

Linda

Of all the Pan-American Exposition attendees with whom to collide, why did it have to be Tommy Rabbit?

Or Tommy Reid. Or whoever he was.

Davey and Dante had been jabbering like bluejays about Tommy Rabbit all week, and the excitement about him had spread throughout the whole house by the weekend. All the boys admired his contributions to the strike in Manhattan, Angelina developed a crush despite never laying eyes on him, and Nina was desperate to meet him. Even the walk to the Pan was dedicated to guessing whether they might see him, by the by. It was a cruel irony that led Linda, and Linda alone, to be face to face with him once again.

That, and the appearance of that strange man.

When she first spied him buying a beer, the hairs on the back of her neck raised. She could've sworn it was her former fiancé, Edward. But last she'd heard, he was married to his former secretary and living in Albany, three hundred miles from Buffalo.

Then she caught the man's eye, they faced each other, and trepidation fixed Linda's shoes to the spot. When he was still in her life, Edward was without a doubt the most classically handsome and polished man she'd ever laid eyes on. For six long, glorious months, they were each other's whole world. Looking at his doppelgänger then, she felt like Alice having stepped through the looking glass. She was staring at an impossible, dark reflection of Edward—a specter. For a moment, she'd been overwhelmed with pity. *What happened to you?*

The people and attractions around her became a blur of color. Sounds were muffled as though they were being played off a record player on the opposite end of the house.

He stepped towards her, and when she realized that her family had proceeded through the fair without her—had forgotten her entirely, it seemed—she ran like all possessed.

The feeling that she was going to die was Linda's steadfast companion as she weaved through the crowd. It stayed with her, too, after she crashed into Tommy, and when Edward's lookalike's hold prevented her from reaching her hatpin, the lone object on her person she could think to use as a makeshift weapon.

Now she was in the middle of the Esplanade—the heart of the Pan, and what must be the busiest plaza this side of the Mississippi—and with no way of knowing where her family had gone.

Something was shoved into her hands. A piece of fabric? She looked down.

A handkerchief. Tommy's.

And now that her tears had been acknowledged, they began to flow in earnest. Her whole body shook. If someone had told her she'd passed through the gates of hell instead of the gates to the Pan-American Exposition, Linda would've believed it.

The details of Edward's abandonment—which were long ago bound and gagged and shoved into the darkest recesses of her mind—now demanded her full attention. Dabbing the corners of her eyes, she recalled oxygen's sudden scarcity when she opened the envelope left on her front stoop a year ago. Every hope of easing her parents' burden and a home of her own was shredded to pieces as easily as her mother ripped the letter itself in her fury.

Tommy gave her a half-smile as she passed back the handkerchief. "There, that's better, ain't it? Letting it all out, I mean. You want to tell me what happened?"

Linda sniffled, then took a breath to gather herself. "I knew that man. Well, someone like him, anyway."

"You know that scalawag?" Tommy's eyes popped open. "He looked like he'd had a cup too much, and it's not quite midday. How in all creation did *you* get to be tied up with *that*?"

Linda grimaced. Really, hadn't she been humiliated enough for one day? "I'd rather not discuss it, if it's all the same to you. Besides, I should be …"

She trailed off, anxiety grabbing hold of her vocal cords. Where *should* she be headed? Her family was still discussing what the plans were for the day when the false Edward materialized. Nothing was set in stone, and—stupidly—they didn't talk about what one ought to do if they separated. Would the safest bet be to walk in the direction they'd been going, or to stay put? Which directions were those, again?

And what if Edward's doppelgänger found her again?

Tommy's brow furrowed. "What's the matter?"

She sighed. "I have no clue where I might find my family again."

"Not to worry, not to worry," Tommy said, brown eyes glistening. "I think I know just how to handle this. We'll take a stroll together, you and me, and—"

"Absolutely not. We can't walk together unattended."

Tommy pulled a face, and Linda realized it was because he was trying to hold back laughter. Laughter!

"Just because *you* don't give a hoot about acceptable ways to behave in public—"

"Hey," Tommy cut her off. "I wouldn't go that far. I just find it a little peculiar that someone so strong and independent, who holds a job *and* walks home every day without a chaperone, is so quick to insist we'd need one now."

Linda narrowed her eyes. "How do you know I walk home without a chaperone *every* day?"

She'd caught him. Tommy clammed right up. She knew she'd felt his eyes on her the past few days during the walk home. She told Aggie and the boys she couldn't be feeling all-overish for no reason, but they'd only teased that Linda only wanted Tommy to be watching her.

She never admitted it to them, but that was entirely probable. Even now, something about Tommy caused gooseflesh to rise across her body. It didn't make a lick of sense. She hardly knew Tommy, and after everything the last personable man in her life had put her through, she didn't want to get to know him.

"All right, I'll tell you what," Tommy said, stroking his chin. "What if you weren't unattended because you're my wife?"

Linda tilted her head. "Surely, I misheard you."

"I'm sure you didn't."

"Mr. Reid, we aren't married!"

"No one has to know that but us. Look around," he replied with a sweeping motion of his arm. "We've been standing here for a while now, and not one person has given us a look, or questioned us about what we're doing. If we can both keep quiet, we could pull the wool over everyone's eyes, and you won't have to worry about running into any other unsavory men."

Linda bit her lip. They *were* at the largest event Buffalo had ever seen. It wasn't like gossiping about them could compare to the main attractions for entertainment. "Perhaps you're right about that, but my parents will have a thousand questions when we find them, and that number will triple when Davey and Dante recognize you."

Tommy winked. "So we won't let them see. Once we spot your family in the crowd, I'll slip into the shadows, and you can just walk right up behind them like you'd been there the whole time."

Something was wrong about his plan. Linda didn't know what it was, but there had to be some reason why she couldn't let herself glide through the Pan with Tommy.

But there wasn't. This was her only option. With a dark Edward doppelgänger on the loose and apparently meaning to do her harm, it wasn't just inappropriate to be traveling alone, but unsafe as well.

And what did Tommy have to gain from this? Nothing that she could see.

Linda sighed in resignation. "All right. You've convinced me."

Beaming, Tommy beckoned her to put her hand around his arm, and reluctantly, she obeyed. "Swell! Now, you don't know where your family is, do you? Had anything on your agenda?"

"We were going to watch my sister perform, but she—"

Tommy gasped. "You mean to say your sister is performing *here*, at the Pan?"

Linda nodded.

"Man alive! Davey and Dante said their sister was a singer, but I didn't know that's what they meant. I suppose that's why you're here—to watch her?"

"Yes. She sings and dances as part of Venice in America, but her show won't start until noon."

Tommy looked up into the sky for a second, then said as casually as anything, "I'd say we have some time, then. Join me for lunch?"

He was getting bolder by the minute, and that was doing strange things to her. Half of the cells in Linda's body wanted her to run, and the other half wanted her to accept the invitation wholeheartedly. He was just being nice, wasn't he? And the way he regarded her—with that hopeful, boyish half-smile—elicited a pleasant shiver down her spine and even managed to get her to smile back at him.

If he did have ulterior motives, he was doing a remarkable job at obscuring them. What he suggested was innocent and safe as could be. They'd be in public the whole time. There wasn't much room for anything to go wrong.

Dear me, he's even more charming than Edward was when we met.

Tommy must've seen her hesitation because he rushed out an explanation. "Well, it's just that I haven't broken my fast yet, and I'm starving. Besides, you're not sure where they'd be right now anyway, right? The Pan is massive." From his pocket, Tommy produced a map, which Linda unfolded. "See? We could walk in circles for a week and not see hide nor tail of them. But that building, the one that's labeled Manufactures and Liberal Arts? They've got free samples of all kinds of foods—enough to fill you up. Or so said one article in the *Express* the other day. Are you hungry?"

"I am, I suppose."

"Then this works out well. You and your family ate your morning meal together, didn't you? So you'll all be peckish around the same time. We could even end up running into them inside if they have the same idea. What do you say?"

It made all the sense in the world. Her family would absolutely come to Nina's performance. They wouldn't miss it for the world. She'd be seeing them shortly. She was just passing the time now, and she happened to be passing it with an attractive, surprisingly well-dressed newsboy. In a handful of hours, she could be back with her parents and her siblings, joining the chorus of praise for their little songbird, Nina. This lunch would be of no consequence.

But if it was of no consequence, why were butterflies taking flight in her stomach?

CHAPTER FIVE

Tommy

Not once did Tommy dream he'd actually encounter Linda doing the Pan. Now he was walking arm and arm with her, and the feeling of awe he experienced when he entered the exposition was nothing in comparison to how wonderstruck he was now.

And after eating with Linda, while circling back towards the Venice in America exhibit, Tommy would keep an eye out for signs of the president. If he could catch his eye now, before he was in front of a podium addressing the hundreds of people present, then he'd be even more likely to listen to his pleas on behalf of working kids.

He could not have planned the day better. The only thing that would make it complete was a little encouragement from Linda.

As they entered the Manufactures and Liberal Arts Building, Tommy glanced at her out of the corner of his eye. Her shoulders were drawn back, and she held herself like she knew every ounce of what she was worth. In New York City, the few girlfriends Tommy had gone with were newsies themselves, and around him, they acted the same as they did while selling papers—coquettish and saccharine. That was the way to sell papers, he supposed—or just his luck—but such sweetness gave him a toothache. Linda might've been a little harsh at times, but she held fast to his arm like she wanted to be there, and before she caught herself, she'd stroked his arm with her thumb. That wasn't the behavior of someone merely putting on an act—no one could see or know it was going on except the two of them.

So Tommy had a spring in his step as they took a turn about the building. In its center, dozens of booths advertised equally as many brand names and foods to try. Attendees gathered in small groups to hear about the health benefits of ginger ale and how many tomatoes went into each of one company's soup can. Steering clear of the latest inventions and fads of tomorrow—fashions, sporting goods, a machine for laundering clothes—Tommy and Linda swiped sandwiches, baked beans, fruit preserves, sponge cake, and mineral waters from three competing companies.

As if knowing his heart's greatest desire, Linda stopped for a moment on their route to sample Welch's unfermented grape juice. "Look, Mr. Reid—that banner says they've got *instant* coffee now. I'd like to try some, wouldn't you?"

Instant coffee? Sharing the aforementioned coffee with her? He paused for a moment to settle his giddiness before responding. "Yes, I would, but you know, you ought to call me Tommy."

Linda raised an eyebrow. "Because we're married?"

Feeling bold, he replied, "Well, that, and because I'd like it."

Linda was still for a moment, then nodded, her lips pursed. She kept her eyes on the instant coffee.

"If you're uncomfortable—"

"I was actually thinking of asking you something. Why do the newsboys call you Tommy Rabbit?"

Tommy stiffened, and he moved to straighten his hat before responding. "I wasn't expecting that sort of question."

"Well, now, if *you're* uncomfortable—"

Her teasing tone caught him off guard, and Tommy laughed just a bit too loud, attracting notice from a nearby circle of women feasting on samples of clam chowder. He walked them towards the instant coffee booth, but kept them hovering just outside of others' earshot to answer her. "Do you remember how I was telling your little brothers about the strike I was a part of?"

Linda scoffed. "That was all they talked about when we got home."

"Really?" Tommy's heart swelled. They were listening. Good. If his efforts proved unsuccessful, it was nice to know that there were newsies who would come after him who might be equally as willing to take up the cause.

"Mm-hm. To hear them tell it, you were a regular hero."

"Well, don't go making me blush now, Miss Morgana."

Rolling her eyes, Linda said, "By your own rules, you should be calling me by my Christian name. Or at least Mrs. Reid."

The way her mouth snapped shut told Tommy that Linda thought she'd said too much, but that didn't convince him to keep his smile from reaching his eyes. Graciously, he decided to let it go. "I'm awfully sorry. As I was saying, Linda, I was striking for better treatment for newsies. But in the end, we didn't get as good of a deal as some of us—namely, me—had hoped for. I was living with my cousin at the time, and my cuz started talking at supper one night after the strike about having kids—first a boy named Daniel like her husband, she said, then a few girls—and I got the feeling that I was only going to be in the way if I stuck around. So I skipped town, and I've skipped many towns since then."

He hadn't meant to drag down Linda's mood, but her brow was puckered now. "So they call you Tommy Rabbit because you hop from place to place. Here I thought it was something about how quick you were or some such." Her volume sank lower and lower with each word. Her eyes were focused on nothing in particular. "But I know exactly what you mean—how you must have felt. That's dreadful."

Alarm bells rang out in Tommy's mind. She knew how he felt? Why?

"I guess that's why you're doing the Pan," Linda continued, "because with all the exhibits like the Streets of Mexico and Fair Japan, you can hop from place to place for a fraction of the mileage and the price."

"No, no. I haven't told you? I'm not here for the exhibits. I'm here for President McKinley."

Linda raised an eyebrow. "Are you looking to get into politics?"

"In a way. I hear he's going to be meeting with constituents, and I have a bone to pick with him about the way our strike ended."

"Please don't take offense, but what would you expect President McKinley to do about it?"

Lowering his voice to keep the families around them from hearing, Tommy's face grew stern. "Linda, if I can get him to listen and let his heartstrings be tugged for just a few minutes, I want to believe I can convince him to pay attention to the kids working in factories, mines, as newsies—*all* the working kids. I've seen too many of my fellow newsies fall into crime after selling papers. Kid Blink, our fearless strike leader? He's in the mob now." Tommy shook his head. "It's a shame. And I'm not saying I have any solutions, but wouldn't you say something ought to be done, so we can promise these kids a future without needing to steal or cheat, or one without mangled limbs in the case of the ones working with machines? Your little brothers and sister included, of course."

Linda stilled. Before Tommy could ask what she was thinking, a man wearing a Kato Coffee Company apron walked up beside them holding out two ceramic mugs. "Have you tried the new *instant* coffee, straight from Chicago? Because who has the time to wait, right? You'll think it's the real thing, and that's a guarantee. Take these and bring them back to me when you're done, and because you two lovebirds look so sweet together, we'll get you a second cup! How does that sound?"

With really no other options, Tommy and Linda politely took the mugs and accepted the egregious wink in their direction as the Kato Coffee Company representative heel-toed back to the safe grounds.

"I detest when they pop up like that," Linda whispered behind the rim of her cup.

"Me, too." Her honesty refreshed Tommy more than the coffee, which hadn't properly been stirred. He'd be lucky to have the bitter taste and the leftover particles out of his mouth before January. By the way her mouth puckered and her nose twitched, Linda was equally disgusted. He leaned a little closer, keeping his eyes off of the Kato Coffee Company booth. "You know, perhaps that slower coffee is worth the wait."

Linda's hand flew to her mouth to suppress a giggle, but it was too late. Not only was the Kato Coffee Company representative looking their way, but she'd already entranced Tommy. Her laugh was lower in pitch than he expected, but it shook her whole body to keep it contained. His smile in reply was automatic, unthinking.

And when she was once again calm, he was instantly flooded with an urge to turn back time and listen to it again. But something she said hadn't yet stopped nagging him. "Is it my turn to ask you a question?"

"I guess so."

"What did you mean earlier when you said you knew how I felt?"

Linda tucked a piece of hair behind her ear. "I don't remember. What were we talking about?"

"Feeling in the way and skipping town."

"Oh." Linda's face fell, and she dragged her finger around the rim of the mug. "Did I say that? I don't know what I was thinking. But a second cup of coffee—good coffee, of course—might jog my memory. Do you think we might be able to make it to the next booth over without incident if we quietly set our mugs down and walk on by?"

There was a story there, too. Tommy ached to uncover it, but he could feel that now was not the time. *Maybe soon*, he dared to hope. "I think you're asking for quite a lot, but I do want more coffee."

Linda took his arm again, and they strolled at an angle that would've taken them towards the exit. At the last second, after setting down their mugs without a glance in the Kato Coffee Company representative's direction, they would pivot to stop at

Maxwell House's booth, too far away to be called back in a way that didn't seem obnoxious.

But, oh, how they woefully misjudged the shrewdness of Kato Coffee Company. Ten paces away, the same representative waved them down. "There are my two favorite lovebirds! Back for another already, huh?"

There was nothing to be done. Basic decency forced polite smiles on Tommy and Linda's faces, and each gracefully accepted another round of the worst-tasting coffee either of them had ever swallowed in their lives.

"So, what have you all done at the Pan so far? I hear there's a dark ride east of here that is very cozy. Or have you already taken a trip? I see those red faces, so don't be coy, don't deny! I know young love when I see it."

Was this an ambush? Tommy watched the color drain from Linda's face as she slowly took back her arm and swayed just a few inches away from him. She held her refilled cup with both hands, as if that was her excuse for uncoupling. Those were the only indications that she'd heard a word the man said. Instead of inventing answers, she blew on her coffee and asked, "Do you have the time?"

"Of course I do, madam." The representative took out a brass pocket watch from somewhere under the apron, checked it, then dropped it back inside. "It's a quarter to one in the afternoon."

Linda almost dropped her cup. "We'll miss Nina's entire performance!"

Tommy set his own untouched cup back on the table. "Thank you for your kindness and the midday pick-me-up, but we must be going."

Together, they flew towards the exit.

CHAPTER SIX

Linda

The Midway—which claimed to house representatives of civilizations from across the world—was one of the most popular gathering places for curious families doing the Pan, and the Venice in America exhibit within it was no exception. Folks gathered along the exhibit's own sliver of the canal to watch gondolas drift by and admire the Palladian architecture meant to mimic Italian villas, with their stucco walls and red roof tiles. Beyond the views, the canal's waters also cooled the breeze, and those who stopped to rest were persuaded to stick around by talented performers like Nina.

That popularity was exactly what frustrated Linda now. She could hear her little sister's mellifluous soprano carried on the wind, but it took many "beg pardons" and a few subtle elbows from Tommy before Linda could catch a glimpse of her sister.

But, oh, what a sight! Nina kept her costume at the Pan, so Linda hadn't seen her all dolled up in her white lace, but there she was! Her long hair flowed down her back in well-groomed ringlets, and her dress was all white lace and delicacy, innocence and sweetness. As onlookers cooed and tossed their coins, Linda's heart felt like it might burst in her chest from pride.

When she'd finally placed herself in the front of the crowd, Linda curtsied, a secret greeting she and Nina had practiced the night before. She watched Nina's eyes find her and light up while an Italian lullaby floated from her mouth in perfect pitch, then returned the curtsy. The act was so darling, coins in larger denominations started to fly over Linda's head.

Linda turned to Tommy to share in her joy, but he looked more puzzled than anything else. "What's the matter?"

"Well, I don't want to ruin this for you."

"Oh, come on now. Tell me."

Tommy sighed and rubbed the back of his neck. "It's just that this is what I was talking about before. How old is she, seven?"

"Nine."

"*Nine* years old, and performing for pocket change?"

She knew he meant no offense, but Linda still felt her cheeks grow hot. "She's not *just* performing for pocket change. She's had paid performances at the concession and the Italian Theatre, too. She loves to sing, and she's extraordinarily talented. And besides," Linda added in a hushed tone, "our family could use the money. If she enjoys the work and she can find it, why shouldn't she use her gifts?"

Tommy shrugged. "I don't know. It reminds me of my newsies. She's working hard, and even though it looks all fun from here, I'm sure it knocks her out, doesn't it? And what would happen if she fell off the gondola, or if singing all day like this hurt her throat or something?" He shook his head. "You're right, she has a great voice, but I'd hate for a job when she's young like this to affect her life after. There's nothing more tragic than that."

She believed him. The sadness in his eyes said it all. Linda's mouth twisted as she considered the possibility. Nina was already being called by reporters a girl with a bright future performing opera. It was impossible to conceive of a world in which Nina Morgana, her little songbird, would not dazzle the world with her singing.

"Nina's your favorite, isn't she?"

Linda nodded. "She's everyone's favorite, I think."

"But she's not the reason you feel in the way?"

Wincing, Linda realized she shouldn't have asked about his nickname back at the Manufactures and Liberal Arts Building.

It was an innocent question; she really was curious. But the discussion that followed opened her up to the same line of questioning, and she couldn't avoid answering twice.

It would help if she didn't want to answer his questions.

Curse his expressive face! It made it so easy to see that he was actually listening to her when she spoke. Not in a waiting-his-turn way, but in a focused, genuine kind of way. And that was more than she could say for most of the adults in her life, with the exception of Aggie.

Linda allowed herself until the end of Nina's song to formulate a response. After Nina belted out the last note and the gondolier began steering Nina towards land, Linda said, "None of my siblings ever made me feel that way. But my parents are another story."

"Why's that?"

Linda looked at him. Could she trust him with this family secret? She hadn't even told Aggie the full extent of her woes, nor Edward when he was still in her life.

Tommy must have sensed the weight of it all on her shoulders. "Maybe that's enough questions from me for the moment, hm?"

"No, no, I'll answer. I—goodness, I don't know how to answer. Where to begin?" Linda fingered the neckline of her dress. "Let's step off to the side. I think Nina will be coming out to greet soon, and we'll just overwhelm her if we try to get her attention while all the strangers are calling for autographs from 'Baby Patti.'"

With a small, understanding smile, Tommy took her hand, and they walked to the point where the smaller canal in front of the Venice in America exhibit met the larger canal that wound its way around the main pavilions, keeping away from the bridge. There was just enough movement and chatter there to provide privacy for their conversations, but not enough to overwhelm the ear or the eye.

Linda swallowed. "My father was a tomcat in Italy. My mother, too, was—a more agreeable word fails me, so I'm just going to say it, all right? Unchaste."

Tommy's slow little nod told her that, from that detail alone, he could guess the rest of the story. But she wanted to tell him more, so she did.

"So, Papà was a tomcat, but he did truly and desperately fall in love with Mamma. She was less enamored of him than he was of her, I think, and then they found out they were expecting me. And—it sounds awful, I know—I don't believe she wanted me." Linda's voice cracked as she forced out the words, but she refused to silence herself. "She would've preferred to have more fun before I was born. But Papà wanted me, and no one in her family or his would have borne anything other than a swift marriage and my birth into a fully-realized family. Now I'm a reminder of her lost years, I suppose. Mind you, all this is what I've gleaned from conversations and the like. They've never told me outright. But I have put enough pieces together to guess at the full picture."

Tommy held out his hands palm side up. When Linda did nothing, he squeezed them into fists and relaxed them again. It was an invitation.

If they were on the streets of New York City—or perhaps if they were in private—she imagined he might take her into his arms to comfort her. She'd bet his arms were strong from hauling around all those newspapers day in and day out. *What would such arms feel like around me?*

And that thought, for a moment, bound her hands to her sides. If they touched, she'd let herself be pulled in, or else pull him towards her first.

But in the next moment, Linda gave in to the temptation and placed her hands on top of his. His affectionate squeeze had the lightest pressure in the world, yet she still felt as though her skin was on fire. Tingles on the tips of her fingers from their contact spread to a full-body warmth. Both serenity and exhilaration filled her at once, yet without contradicting each other.

She looked into his eyes and forgot all.

"Lindy! *Lindy!*"

Nina's voice brought Linda out of the moment, and she took her hands back to turn around and embrace her little sister, planting a dozen kisses on top of her head, murmuring compliments between pecks while Nina squealed with glee. When Linda was satisfied with how much affection she'd shown, she took a step back and gestured to Tommy. "Nina, this is Mr. Thomas Reid. This is the man David and Dante call Tommy Rabbit."

Nina curtsied and put on what she called her "grown-up voice." "It's a pleasure to meet you, Mr. Rabbit."

Chuckling, Tommy bowed in response.

With introductions out of the way and most of the crowd dissipated, Nina reverted back to her true self, bouncing in her little white, high-heeled shoes. "I'm so glad you're here! And I'm starved. Where are Mamma and Papà and everyone else?"

Linda frowned. "You don't mean you haven't seen them?"

"They probably just ran off to buy you ice cream, that's all," Tommy said, rescuing both Linda and Nina's good moods. "And if I'm wrong, I'll get you a bowl of the stuff myself. How's that sound?"

Nina shook her head as she held out one of her hands and opened to reveal eight shiny quarters. "That's nice, but you don't need to. I can buy *so much ice cream* with the money I got from singing."

"Now that's a gal after my own heart," Tommy said with a smile in Linda's direction. "She's got a good head on her shoulders and she's practically made of money."

"So can we get ice cream, Lindy?" Nina asked, pushing out her lower lip.

Linda gave Tommy a glance that was meant to say, *Now look what you've done*. He only tossed his hands up in the air, as if the whole thing was out of his control.

Linda might've even agreed to get Nina a treat—after all, the rest of their family was nowhere to be found anyway—but a chill raked down her spine and froze her blood, stealing away all other thoughts.

No, not again. Not with Nina here.

But yes, it was that dark twin of Edward's who was crossing over the bridge and headed right for them.

CHAPTER SEVEN

Tommy

It took Tommy a moment to recognize Linda's previous attacker. For one thing, he was looking much more drunk now, having taken the full half of a day to order as many alcoholic beverages as he pleased. His appearance had taken a turn for the worse as well, with his shirt untucked and his shoelaces flinging every which way as he stumbled over to them. Now, instead of looking like only a madman, he looked downright pitiable.

"Hey, I just want to talk to you," were the first slurred words out of his mouth.

Before he'd gotten through the first syllable, Linda had pulled Nina's arm and arranged her to stand behind. "What could you possibly want?"

Nina peered up at Tommy from behind Linda. "What's happening?"

Tommy put a finger up to his lips.

"I was wrong to leave you in the dust like that," he said, his eyes half-lidded. "It's okay. We can make up. I want to be with you. Come home with me, honey."

Linda glared at him, then turned back to Tommy. "Take Nina."

The drunk's knees twitched like he might fall to the ground at any second, and he threw out his arms akimbo. By Tommy's estimation, he was a shell of a man, and he posed no real threat now that he'd lost his sense of balance.

And Linda? Wow, could Linda ever handle herself. She was

formidable. And her fierce protection of her little sister warmed Tommy's heart.

But there were other things to focus on. A restaurant sat just on the other side of the bridge. Tommy waved over Nina. "Why don't you and me get that ice cream we were talking about while Linda and this fellow have a chat?"

Nina hesitated.

"Come on, Nina. You can tell me about what your house is like, huh? And what other songs you like to sing."

"No, I want to stay with Lindy."

"I know, little lady, but—"

The drunk's voice was now booming, drowning out Tommy and drawing the eye of every passerby within twenty paces. "Why can't you just be a good girl and come talk about it, huh? We can talk about it!"

Linda was rapidly losing her composure, and she looked hardly able to believe she was having the present conversation. "No, we really cannot. You need to go. Now."

Again, Tommy motioned for Nina to cross the bridge with him. Again, Nina refused.

The argument raged on. "Is it because of *that* man?"

Tommy and Linda's eyes met for one fleeting moment. Then Linda hissed, "Leave them out of it, you masher."

His features weren't working well enough to form a real smile, but the corners of his mouth did their best to turn upward. "Say, I know that guy. Think he sold me a newspaper. You like the, uh, newspaper boy better than me?" The drunk was much better at imitating a scowl. "Why? *I* have a *real* job. I'm better than that cad, that overgrown guttersnipe!"

Now that he was good and angry, the drunk slogged towards Linda. This time, she was ready for him. In one swift and frightening movement, Linda plucked out her hatpin, stepped out at an angle, and held the pin level with his throat. If he fell forward or tried to grab at Linda, Tommy had no doubt that she'd skewer his Adam's apple.

Tommy grabbed hold of Nina and covered her eyes while he watched, spellbound.

Linda's voice was colder and steelier than the metal in her hand. "Get out of here."

The drunk stood his ground. Tommy was almost impressed with him. Linda was absolutely terrifying in this state, and he would've fled as soon as he'd caught sight of the hatpin glinting in the sunlight. He'd skimmed plenty of articles detailing robbers and ruffians who'd messed with the wrong woman and found themselves repeatedly punctured. A woman with a hatpin could be lethal.

"I'm warning you!"

The drunk took a half-step closer, his hand outstretched, and Linda jabbed the hatpin forward. She missed piercing his flesh by a fraction of an inch—a warning.

And now that he'd seen how close he was to injury, the drunk was sweating and shaking. Tommy was, too. If the drunk tried anything Linda couldn't predict, it might only be a few seconds and luck that decided which of them would wind up impaled. Even Nina, as if she could sense the tension, was completely still and silent.

If he lays a hand on you, Linda, I'll knock him out cold, Tommy repeated in his head like a prayer.

Before things could go any further, from some ways away, a man's voice roared in a language Tommy didn't understand.

Nina gasped and pushed away Tommy's hands. "Papà!"

Linda and Nina's family—both parents and all six of their siblings—were charging up the street. Realizing he was about to have more trouble on his hands than he knew what to do with, the drunk pulled foot for the opposite end of the Pan.

When Tommy got a glimpse of Linda's parents' faces, he got an itch to flee, too. Mr. Morgana was stout and sure-footed, and his outrage was plain on his face. The same was true for Linda's mother, who was glowering at Tommy as though willing him to spontaneously catch fire.

Poor Nina was left perturbed from the encounter with the drunk, and she ran to the safety in the comfort of her mother's arms. "Mamma, that man was so scary!"

Oh, Miss Nina, why'd you have to go and word it like that?

Mrs. Morgana regarded Tommy the way someone might have reacted to a large spider or cockroach. "What did you say to her?"

"It wasn't Tommy who scared Nina," Linda clarified. "It was the man who just took off. He tried to attack me."

The siblings erupted with questions, which all flowed from their mouths at once. It sounded like a bunch of noise to Tommy, but Linda shushed them and passed out answers like pieces of candy. "Yes, I'm all right. We're all fine. He was just someone with an illness, Angelina, no one any of us know. Nina sang wonderfully in the show, and I'm sorry you all missed it. Yes, Joseph, that's Tommy Rabbit."

Tommy waved as the Morgana siblings rushed up to him to tug on his shirt and coat, and a most uncharacteristic shyness overcame him. He looked up at Linda, who was pressing her lips together to hold back a laugh, and decided he didn't mind the onslaught so much.

Mrs. Morgana called each of her children out by name in such a way that you couldn't tell where one began and another ended. "Come. We're moving on."

Everyone groaned, but they obeyed, trailing behind the elder Morganas as they marched in the direction from which they came. Tommy tensed as Linda turned to go, but then she paused, her eyes unfocused.

"Mamma," Linda called out, "I'll be there in a moment."

Mrs. Morgana gave only a wave as indication she'd heard Linda. That alone spoke volumes to Tommy. They'd only just reunited after being separated for half the day, and they'd just seen her fending off someone who clearly meant her harm. How could a mother give her child the cold shoulder like that? Even if Linda's parents were being kept busy with a hundred of her siblings instead of just six—or five, since Nina had been performing—he would've expected either of her parents to tell them where to meet with her, where they were going—*something*.

Linda cast her eyes downward as she put her hatpin back into place. "Well, Mr. Reid, thank you for returning me to my family, and for a nice lunch with pleasant company. I believe this is where we part ways."

Tommy's mouth fell open just a little. He was struck by the pain that coursed through him on behalf of this woman who, to most anyone else, would've been considered a mere acquaintance.

Maybe he should've only thought of her as such. It was only their second time meeting, and they were only just getting to know each other. But everything in Tommy rebelled at the application of logic to their relationship. His affection for her couldn't be explained by mere infatuation, and a connection so unusual and strong begged to be pursued.

"I don't get it. Just like that, our day's over? After all we've shared and done?"

Linda's cheeks reddened. "Well, what did you expect?"

An invitation to join you, or a promise to find me later. I'd like a kiss goodbye, too. "I don't know, but I figured this wasn't the end. Will I see you again?"

"You're still a newsboy, aren't you? As are my little brothers." Her smile was meant to be warm, but she hadn't thrown all of her effort behind it, and something sadder peeked through the cracks. "And I'm still a typist at the *Buffalo Express*. I'm sure our paths will cross again."

"Well, sure, they'll cross, but will we see each other like this again? Do you even *want* to see me? Because if you don't, Linda, just say the word, and you'll never catch hide nor tail of me again."

For a while, Linda said nothing. The silence would've only lasted a few seconds, but to Tommy, the quiet stretched to fill days, during which he contemplated where this had all gone wrong. Should he have been more forward, told her how being next to her and talking about that disgusting, bitter instant coffee was the easiest conversation he'd ever had? Should he have insisted on walking her home the day they met, and then maybe she would be singing a different tune now?

Or maybe he shouldn't have gotten his hopes up in the first place. Just because he was enamored with her didn't mean she felt the same way. He'd figured her distance was just nerves or extreme caution, but what if she just didn't like him?

Why would she like an overgrown newsie anyway? He couldn't provide for her on his meager income, and he didn't have any other skills to speak of that might help him land something better. He was a dead-end road.

Linda sighed. "I don't know what I want, Tommy. But I have to go. That must've been so frightening for Nina. She needs me. They all need me. And ... And you have to meet with President McKinley soon, don't you?"

"I guess so."

"Well, there you go," Linda said as she took a few steps backwards. "I'll be seeing you next week, I suppose. If you're still in Buffalo and haven't hopped away before then, that is."

He could tell she meant it playfully, but in the moment, hopping away didn't sound so bad to Tommy. If distance could in any way dampen the sour, terrible pain of Linda's not-quite-rejection, he'd cross oceans the same night. They'd had such a nice time together. He thought he'd grown on her.

But if he was wrong—if she hadn't had a nice time, and if the laughs and confessions they shared weren't enough to endear her to him—what else could he do but let her go?

"Maybe," Tommy muttered, his nerve lost. "You might not, but I don't know. Maybe."

Tommy's mind was so fuzzy, he didn't have the sense to send her off like a gentleman. He could only stare as her figure receded in the distance and then be swallowed by her family and the crowds, and wonder why he did such a damned foolish thing as letting Linda Morgana steal his heart.

CHAPTER EIGHT

Linda

On the heels of the hardest thing she'd ever had to do in her life, Linda was bombarded by her younger siblings with ten thousand questions. Every one of them was jealous that she got to spend part of the day with Tommy Rabbit. All except for Nina, who was happy to answer all of their questions on Linda's behalf, having spent the past several minutes with him, which was more than any of the others could say.

So far, Linda agreed with every point Nina made. He was kind, he was funny, and he did smell like newspapers and earth.

But Nina was missing a few adjectives, wasn't she? Tommy was also good with children, intelligent, and strong in every way. Not to mention handsome. Now that she'd had ample time to observe his features, Linda found them more and more pleasing until just a glance in her direction did a number on her heart. Linda admired him, too, for his ambitious nature. She wished she'd talked about that with him a little more. Who else would—after what most of the world considered a successful strike—decide to spend hard-earned dollars attempting to speak to *the President of the United States himself* to bring attention to the everyday injustices?

The more she thought about Tommy as she and her family looped around to traipse up the Midway, the more her stomach ached with guilt and regret. But what could she possibly say after she was so frigid towards him? Passing him on the streets on her walk home from work now would make her self-conscious, and she could imagine he might be just plain humiliated. She considered her mental map of Buffalo's streets and thought of a couple alternative routes, but in truth, she didn't have any desire to take them. She wanted to see him again.

But what had he meant by *maybe* he'd be seeing her? She was only poking fun at him, but did she take his suggestion that he leave town seriously?

"And *then*, after the Pan," Nina continued, breaking her momentum to take a cartoonishly deep breath, "I'm going to become a newsgirl, and we can all become newsboys and newsgirls, and Tommy Rabbit can teach us how to sell papers properly. We'll be rich!"

Speaking in his native Italian, their father asked Linda what Nina and the others were so excited about. Linda translated, and he grunted in reply. "The girl needs to focus on her singing. We've paid good money for the lessons. And the boys shouldn't get so absorbed in her fantasies."

Linda bristled. The younger children spoke mostly English at school and to each other, but it wasn't like they'd forgotten Italian entirely. Children were *supposed* to be absorbed in fantasies.

Linda leaned towards Angelina and whispered for her to take the children up closer to the ostrich farm they were passing by. Once they were far out of earshot, Linda turned to her father. "They're just excited to have met Tommy Rabbit. He's really a good man. I think you'd like him if you spoke with him."

"*That* was this revolutionary Tommy Rabbit fellow none of them will stop talking about? He's too old to be selling newspapers. That's a job for little boys."

"I think he likes the work, Papà," Linda said, feeling the need to tread carefully. "And he's quite good at it."

He eyed her. "Grown men are also good at tying their shoelaces. That doesn't mean it's a respectable living. Concetta, did you know about this?"

Linda's mother tsked and rolled her eyes. "I knew. Why do you think he didn't receive an invitation to dinner? I don't want him putting any other ridiculous thoughts in my children's heads."

"Mamma, you're talking about the man who escorted me around all day while I was lost," Linda said more sharply than she'd ever spoken in her life, "and I must say, I had the most wonderful—"

"Is *that* what happened?" Her mother shook her head, and her eyes were all fire. "I thought his presence was a coincidence. I should've known better. You ran off and flirted all day with that good-for-nothing, didn't you? In the future, if you're going to be leaving your family to throw your good reputation away, at least fall into the arms of a man who has money to help your family. I think I'd rather you take a second look at Edward Gallagher than someone who goes by the name Tommy Rabbit."

Linda bit her tongue until she tasted pennies to keep herself from objecting. Her parents preferred Edward Gallagher, the two-timing snake who shattered her life's plans, to someone who truly made her happy? What could they be thinking?

Before she could find her words, Davey broke away from his siblings and walked back over to Linda and their parents. Deaf to the grown-ups' conversations, he asked, "Mamma, where are we going again?"

"After we get a little food in your sister at that little restaurant, we're going to the Temple of Music. It's just up ahead."

Davey chimed in, "But why again?"

"Because that's where the President is speaking. I won't be answering those questions again, so you'd better commit the answers to memory this time."

Had she heard that correctly? A warm glow that began in her chest spread throughout Linda's body. Tommy would be there. She could see him. She could apologize for brushing him off and—

Linda's father interrupted her daydreams. "And then we're going home."

"But why?" Linda asked a little too excitedly.

"Because we've done plenty for one day, with you getting yourself lost and all of us getting shoved around by all these people. And I need a nap."

And I need to clear the air with Tommy. Linda put on her sweetest smile. "Well, you know, I did want to stay, if that's all right. I can take the children off your hands for a little while longer. Angelina and I could take the others around to see the other attractions—I've seen lots of women my age running around the Pan without any chaperone, so I think it would be all right. Or, Mamma, if you wanted to stay—"

"It's not *just* your father who's exhausted. We all are. Dante looks moments from collapsing as it is." She added under her breath, "I do know we wouldn't be so tired if you helped us manage the younger ones like you promised us at home."

But I always help with the younger ones, Linda almost said. Her parents knew that, though. They knew, and they didn't care. She was their spinster servant-daughter. If she must abandon that label, then she would be the eldest daughter they married off to the first man of means who would have her. They didn't care about her the way parents should—either because they didn't have the energy, or because she was the result of rash decisions made in their youth, and they figured they'd already fulfilled their obligations to her by allowing her a chance to walk the earth.

She and Tommy wouldn't have followed in those footsteps. Not in a million years. Whatever or *whoever* came along, they would make the most of it. That's the sort of spirit Tommy embodied. She liked that about him, and thought she could use more of that in her life. In fact, she liked Tommy a lot, even if she spent the entire time they were together hiding that fact from him and herself. And he liked her, too. They would've been happy if she let them have a real chance. Dirt poor, perhaps, but happy.

Too bad she'd made sure that chance at happiness was crushed underfoot before she walked away from him.

But perhaps all was not lost. She would only know for sure if that was the case at the Temple of Music.

CHAPTER NINE

Tommy

Tommy wouldn't have walked any slower or with more effort than if he was wearing leaden shoes. Hearing Linda suggest that he might beat a hasty retreat from Buffalo before he saw her again just ripped him in half the way nothing else could have. Sure, that's how he'd gotten the nickname Tommy Rabbit, but what made her think he was going to get out of town so quickly after doing the Pan?

Was that what she wanted to happen?

He shook his head. Focusing on Linda was not going to help him now. As much as he didn't want to, he needed to let her go because there was something more important that needed his attention.

The time to confront President McKinley was growing near.

After another walk through the Manufactures and Liberal Arts Building—narrowly avoiding the overzealous instant coffee peddlers—Tommy approached the Temple of Music caffeinated and, at the sight of the building, intimidated. The Temple of Music was even more ornate than the Electric Tower, the alleged crown jewel of the Pan. Blood red was the primary accent color used in decoration, and its effects were even greater when paired with the backdrop of ivory and gold.

Tommy had never set foot into such a regal-looking structure. He felt immediately that he didn't belong there, and watching the number of people who crowded into the auditorium as "The Star-Spangled Banner" flooded his ears didn't help. Of course,

Tommy had been battling against hordes of people all day, and he was somewhat used to being one misstep away from getting trampled in the streets.

But all that had taken place outdoors. Now that he was inside, the hundreds of people pressed together gave the illusion that Tommy was in the middle of the largest crowd of his life, and for a moment, he froze. This was a million times different than the only possible experience he could've compared this to in his head—the newsies' union rally. But there, he'd been surrounded by peers. Now he met eyes with absolute strangers, and without a newspaper to sell or a headline to bark, he felt awkward and useless.

You're not here for them, Tommy reminded himself. *You're here for McKinley. Find McKinley.*

Tommy circled the perimeter of the room. Mostly, he was searching for the President, but the walking also helped Tommy think. The room was abuzz with commentary on what everyone had planned to say to McKinley, or what they just finished chatting about with him. Snippets of conversations drifted towards Tommy's ears during his lap.

"It's so nice that the leader of our country makes time to talk to us average folks."

"President McKinley told me that this was his favorite part of being a politician—meeting the people."

"He said the same thing to me. Shame his schedule won't let him share more than ten minutes with all of us."

Tommy's heartbeat thundered in his ears. He had no idea he'd have so little time.

There he is.

President William McKinley stood in the dead center of the auditorium. Now that he'd spotted him, Tommy felt a little silly for not identifying him earlier. McKinley was the most formally attired man in the room, with a black silk top hat that shook with him when he laughed.

Tommy was going to have to interrupt his good time. For that, he felt a little guilty, but he forced one foot in front of the other anyway. No one else was going to do this but him. Hundreds of newsies had lived through selling papers as a child on the streets and lived to tell about it as an adult, and no one had come to their rescue yet. Then, he watched McKinley bend down to a young girl's level to give her the red carnation pinned to his lapel, and Tommy thought he might actually have a chance at getting McKinley to listen.

He took it as a sign. Gritting his teeth and gripping his pant legs, Tommy resolved to confront McKinley for the newsies, the factory workers, the miners, everybody who suffered as a plaything of the greedy and powerful. To do it for Clancy McCoy, and Davey and Dante Morgana.

A part of him wished Linda could be there to share in the moment, or at least to help loosen the knots in his stomach. He pushed her out of his mind again.

As Tommy approached, a second, older man gripping a handkerchief like the devil began to walk towards McKinley from the other side of the room. Tommy did not initially give the man a second glance. He was too wrapped up in rehearsing his wording. *Pleased to meet you, Mr. President. If I could have a moment of your time later*—No, all that would take too long to say. *Mr. President, you must take action on child labor. There are little girls like the one with your carnation dying in your country's streets!* No, that was bleak to the point of sounding unhinged.

He was almost to McKinley, but the other man was stepping a little lighter, and he'd get to the President first. *All right, I'll position myself to be the very next person he sees.*

Being so focused on his agenda, Tommy didn't hear the gunshots. What he actually heard first was a high-pitched ringing, like a fly in his ear, but immeasurably more unpleasant. The older man with the handkerchief was thrown to the ground by one, then two, then five or six men.

Tommy couldn't make sense of what he was witnessing. Spinning around, he watched every visitor stampeded towards the exits as outsiders tried to make their way into the Temple of Music to see what was going on. Wordless screams and calls for help in every pitch echoed throughout the auditorium, causing the red curtains to vibrate and Tommy's blood to turn to ice water. He needed to move, but whatever fears had tried and failed to paralyze him before transmogrified into ghoulish new ones, grew to be ten times their size and weight, then redoubled their efforts to keep Tommy planted to the ground.

It couldn't be what Tommy thought. It just couldn't be. He couldn't conceive of it. There had to be some other reason why McKinley had staggered backwards like that, and why he was being helped into a chair by three people.

"You!" A man with a short boxed beard in a nondescript suit—*Secret Service*, Tommy's mind whispered to him—shoved a finger in Tommy's face. "What are you standing there for? What do you know?"

His words couldn't find their way off the tip of his tongue. But he'd seen that all-fired look in the eye before—in the glares from cops during the strike. Even if Tommy could speak, it might not have done him any good. The men who thought of themselves as protectors had suffered a loss, and just like anybody when things went horribly wrong, they were trying to recover order any way they could.

"What do you know about this? What do you know about that guy?"

Tommy followed the bearded man's pointing finger until he'd found the man with the handkerchief, the man who shot the President of the United States, lying on the floor. Bruises were already beginning to form from where he'd been beaten with the butt end of rifles to keep from getting away. Even with the shiner, Tommy was sure he'd never seen him before in his life, so he shook his head.

"Fine, don't talk," the bearded man snarled, "but we'll be taking you in anyway until we can get to the bottom of things."

With a hard smack on his shoulder, Tommy was spun around,

and his arms were jerked behind his back. The reality of the situation set in as he heard the click of the cuffs—he was being taken into custody for a crime he had nothing to do with. Beyond that, the crime was *attempted assassination*.

Tommy couldn't yet conceive of the President of the United States having been shot—possibly fatally—right in front of him. But he *could* conceive of not being able to talk with him. He understood that his chance at convincing a powerful member of the government to pay attention to the plights of working children was taken from him.

And in the process, he'd let working children everywhere—especially the newsies—down.

CHAPTER TEN

Linda

With all of Nina's and the others' needs met, the Morgana family strolled towards the Temple of Music like they hadn't a care in the world. All except Linda, who stepped a little more lightly than the others, just a few feet of the ahead of the rest.

"Linda, *passerotta*, slow down," her father pleaded.

"Let her walk ahead," her mother scoffed. "She's old enough to not be babied."

They argued about whether that was actually true, but Linda ignored them. She was so close! If God had any good fortune to spare, he'd let her see Tommy again. He might have some advice for her.

But as Linda took in the majesty of the Temple of Music, her face fell, and then her expression morphed to one of horror. There was chaos and shouting, people running as though being chased.

Her mother held out her arms to stop her children following behind her. "People have lost their minds!"

Linda studied the scene. This wasn't run-of-the-mill mayhem, but she struggled to imagine a suitable catalyst. Luckily, she didn't have to wrestle with her confusion for long. Almost as soon as she resolved to walk up to the next person who looked privy to what went on, an older woman in an elaborate, canary yellow afternoon dress hurried up to them as she fled the Temple of Music, panting. "How are you standing there? Didn't you hear? The President has been shot!"

Her parents exchanged looks. The older Morgana siblings gasped and pummeled the poor woman with questions while their younger counterparts remained mostly quiet and wide-eyed, absorbing. Nina asked, "What's a president?"

As for Linda, she was crawling out of her skin. The President, who they were on their way to see, was either dead or was closer to it. She shuddered as she focused her eyes on the Temple of Music, thinking now that it resembled a grand tomb more than anything else.

It struck her that *she'd* come face to face with her mortality twice earlier the same day. The first time, when Edward's doppelgänger set his sights on her, a primitive part of Linda knew that if she hadn't evaded him, she'd be easily overpowered. Few would have the courage or care to ask whether she was actually supposed to be under his care, as he'd tried to convince Tommy. That was something like the real Edward, except the real Edward's silver tongue was nearly faultless, and he had much more subtle ways of exerting power over her at his disposal.

The second time Edward's doppelgänger found her, however, was not nearly so unnerving—not after Tommy had called her strong and independent, and in doing so brought those traits to her attention. Her threat to run the doppelgänger through with her hatpin proved those points. She would've done it, too, if he'd gotten just a hair closer. That was the kind of boldness that Tommy inspired in her.

But—though Linda wouldn't have admitted it to herself before now—if everything had gone wrong, she would've died having been miserable for most of her life. She did dearly love her siblings, but after a day on her own, she realized she felt more stifled and suffocated by her parents than ever before. And her mother's barbs made it clear that, no matter how perfect she tried to be for them, her parents would still see her as the cause of their downfall.

It was time to be more like Tommy, and take her life into her own hands. Unlike her parents, Linda would not doom herself to a life she didn't want to lead. *I'll stay at Aggie's. Her mother likes me. It won't take me too long to save up. Maybe Aggie would be willing to rent an apartment with me.*

And then, once Linda was settled into a new living space and could pay for her own way of life, she'd look for Tommy, if he was anywhere to be found. No, before then. She could ask Davey and Dante to keep their ears to the ground if he didn't appear outside the *Buffalo Express*. She didn't know what she'd do if they couldn't get a hold of him. Send out telegraphs?

All she knew was that she wanted Tommy Reid in her life. If he was going to continue hopping from place to place like he'd been doing, she wanted to go with him.

Linda placed a delicate hand on her father's shoulder. "Papà, since we won't be visiting the Temple of Music, could I have a word with you in private?"

After several long seconds, he nodded. "Concetta, my love, would you take the children for ice cream while we have this chat?"

All of Linda's siblings cheered, the melancholy surrounding President McKinley getting shot entirely forgotten. Their mother rolled her eyes, but herded them back towards the Midway.

Taking his hand, Linda led her father to a nearby bench. He didn't sit, but slumped onto the chair, removing his hat to run his fingers through his jet black hair. Over the years—he was forty-four now, and he wore every year a little worse—the black had lost some of its luster and sheen. Of course it would be now that Linda also noticed that much of the black had been replaced by gray. *He's fine and all now, but he and Mamma will only get older. How would they manage without me?*

Now that she was sitting beside him, Linda couldn't find her words. How could she possibly phrase this—the proposal of an immense shift in the Morgana family dynamics—without offending or casting a gloom on him? Perhaps she'd acted too quickly on her thoughts.

Her father chuckled without humor. "I thought you wanted a word with me."

"I do, but this is hard. I'm not sure where to begin."

"Does this have anything to do with that Rabbit man?"

Linda pinched herself to keep from smiling. "Yes, Tommy Reid does have something to do with it."

"I knew I didn't like him."

"Papà—"

Her father huffed. "Will you tell me what you wanted to tell me already?"

"I'm *trying*." Linda took his hand in both of hers. "Papà, I think it's time for your eldest bird to fly far from her nest, wouldn't you say?"

A thousand emotions crossed his face before settling on horror. "But what will happen to you? And to us? Where will you go?"

Linda steeled herself, lifting her chin and pushing her shoulders back, like those actions alone might conjure the strength she needed. "Don't fret over me. I have some savings, and if I continue saving a large part of my salary, I'll be able to move with Aggie McCoy into our own room. She has been wanting her own accommodations for some time now, and this is the perfect opportunity. We'll still live in the city, at least for a while. I can visit, but I won't be the maid or the nanny any longer."

Her father's eyes narrowed. "What did that Tommy boy say to you? I would have sworn that was who you were going to announce as your roommate."

"No, no, he didn't say anything I couldn't have figured out for myself. I just needed someone to say it, and he was just the person to open his mouth."

"I see." Her father's tone was gruff, and he wouldn't look her in the eyes. "Your family has been your burden for too long, and you want your freedoms."

Linda scowled. "You know that's not what I'm saying. Why must you twist my words?"

"But it *is* what you're saying, and I don't like it. We've cared for you, provided for you, and this is how you thank us, by casting aside all our wishes for you? I wanted to see you settled and married by now. I wanted to see you at home with my grandchildren!"

"There's no reason that couldn't still happen. I would just be doing it on my own, that's all."

"It's not right for women to live alone. Who'll take care of you?"

"Take care of me?" Indignation swelled in Linda's chest. She crossed her arms as if to smother the feeling. "That's a funny way to look at the past few years of my life. I've provided for *you* financially."

Her father looked incredulous. "You wanted a job! And we agreed to let you because you said it might help you find a husband, and you swore you'd take still care of your brothers and sisters. Now you're saying you'd rather abandon them anyway, not to mention your mother and me, and you're still unmarried."

"I wanted a job because I needed to get out of that house. You made choices that led to you having so many children with not enough time and hardly enough money to feed them. I didn't make those choices, but the consequences were pushed onto me anyway. Tell me how that's fair! Tell me that you wouldn't ask for the same if you were in my place!"

Realizing she was raising her voice now, Linda quieted. She stared at her father, who still hadn't looked at her for some time. There wasn't anger in his face, but something darker and more piercing—heartbreak. He wasn't a cruel man. Distant and brusque, yes, but his sharpness never had the same cutting effects as her mother's.

A large part of her pitied him more than anything.

He took a shaky breath. "There's no changing your mind?"

Linda shook her head.

"Well, it sounds like you have everything worked out." His eyes glazed over, and he shrugged. "Your mother will not be happy, but I suppose I'd rather see you off and know where you're going than trap you with us until you find some other way to escape, since that's the way you feel about things."

Linda rose to her feet, then gave him a peck on the cheek. "Thank you, Papà. This won't have to happen right this minute, but it does have to happen soon. At your very earliest convenience, I'd say." She rubbed his hand and gave his knuckles a kiss as well. "Now, I'm going to walk with you to where Mamma and the others went, then I'm going to go look for Tommy. Last I heard, he was heading to the Temple of Music as well, but I haven't seen him come out of the building. You should still expect me home for supper tonight, and I'll do all my usual chores while under your roof, and my brothers and sisters won't have to know a thing until the details have been worked through. Does that sound fair?"

Stony silence.

"*Papà*, does it?"

"Well, give me a moment to think on what you've said! I don't want you to go, Linda, and I don't think your mother would want you to forgo your duties at home. You know her feelings on what young ladies should do for their mothers. I have half a mind to lock you in your room."

Linda sighed. "Nevertheless, I will be going. I know I'm ready for it, and you can't keep me locked away forever. This is me asking for your blessing, not your permission. Will you or won't you grant it to me?"

A different sort of silence fell over her father, and tears sprang to his eyes. Linda wiped them away as they fell down his cheeks, then ushered him forward to catch up with everyone else, the whole time praying that her discussion with Tommy would go just as smoothly.

If she could find him.

CHAPTER ELEVEN

Tommy couldn't say for sure how long he'd been sitting cuffed and cross-legged on the floor, but the Secret Service agent that eventually came to collect him said they'd determined he probably had nothing to do with it, and that it'd only been a half hour since they took him. *Could've fooled me.*

No sooner had he regained full mobility of his limbs than a reporter—made identifiable by the notepad and pencil in her hands—spotted him from across the room. Tommy braced himself. Despite being in a somewhat symbiotic relationship with reporters as one of the newsies, he tended to avoid them. Something about other people taking notes while he spoke didn't sit right with him. Almost always, he could get out of talking with them because there was someone more interesting or more charismatic around to relay the facts. Not this time. This time, the clacks of the reporter's heeled shoes on the wooden floor were meant for him.

"Excuse me," she said, her voice as clear as a bell, "but are you the young man the Secret Service took into custody in connection to the shooting of President McKinley?"

Tommy nodded. "Did he make it?"

The reporter frowned. "So far, he seems to be doing all right. One of the bullets only grazed him, but the other hit close to his stomach, they think. The ambulance took him away to the Exposition hospital." She stuck out her hand, which Tommy took to shake. "I'm Ellen Endicott—call me Ellen—from the *Buffalo Weekly Courier*. Do you mind if we chat outside? I've gotten all I need from in here, and the agents have been giving me dirty looks."

"Actually, I'm not so sure I'm who you want to talk to."

Her eyebrows jumped up. "Well, *I'm* sure. What makes you think I have the wrong man?"

"It's just—"

"On second thought, let's absquatulate first."

Tommy looked over his shoulder to see an agent staring them down. Careful not to show any signs of being intimidated, he marched towards the door right behind Ellen.

Once they were safely outside and far from listening years, Ellen spun around to face Tommy, her pencil hovering over a fresh sheet on her notepad. "All right, I'm ready. Start with your name and why you don't want to talk to me."

"Well, my name's Thomas Reid."

"Are you the same Thomas Reid from the newsboy strike? Tommy Rabbit, I think you go by?"

Tommy nodded as Ellen made her notes. "That's me. But I wouldn't use those words, exactly—I mean, about not wanting to talk to you."

"So then use your own."

She didn't sound annoyed, but her clipped words infused each sentence with urgency. Tommy felt too rushed to think of anything other than the unvarnished truth. "I've had to talk to a lot of reporters in my day, and it makes me nervous. I don't really talk like a book either, so all the quotes you get from me will sound like you got them from a simpleton." Tommy swallowed to clear the lump in his throat. "But besides all that, I don't even know what I saw in there."

Ellen nodded, her eyes shining with sympathy. "I understand. I've witnessed lots of things I'd rather not speak of again, but think of it this way—you are a key witness to what could be the most important political death of our lifetimes. Now, I'm of the opinion that preserving contemporary events for the history books is one of the single most important acts one can take, but I know not everybody thinks that way. If you'd like, I can find someone else who is inside the Temple of Music at the time. It wouldn't be too hard—after the shock wears off, it'll be all anyone will talk about."

Ellen made a good point. Tommy sighed, then began his tale with entering the Temple of Music and first catching sight of President McKinley. As Tommy spoke, he fell into a rhythm. Soon, he didn't feel like he was talking at all, but instead watching himself talk from a spot above his head. The words didn't feel like his anymore, but they came streaming out of his mouth naturally, like water from a faucet.

Despite the events he was describing getting more and more grim, Ellen's smile only grew wider. As he was wrapping up, Ellen looked up from her feverish scribbling. "Would you say you have a good memory?"

"Yeah, I'd say so."

"And you're observant, you'd say? Do you have good people skills?"

Tommy squinted. "Why do you ask?"

Ellen tapped her pencil against her temple in thought. "Because you've got a good sense of where and how to add the details—only the important ones—and you don't sensationalize. You're essentially writing this story for me now, if I'm being honest with you. I allow that's from reading so many newspapers when you aren't making sales. Still, you've got the makings of a good writer. What do you do for work now?"

Tommy looked down, not sure how to take the compliment. "I still just sell papers. I've sold the *Courier* before, but I mostly sell the *Express*."

Ellen flipped back all the pages in her notepad to retrieve a neat, typewritten business card and hand it to Tommy. "If you don't mind my saying so, it's high-time you earned a little promotion. My paper is always looking for new blood. I don't think becoming an investigative reporter would be too high for your nut one day. And you're a newsie! Even better! You already know what stories move papers!"

"Sure, sure, but I actually was hoping to take more of an active role in things. The whole reason I burned almost every penny I had coming here was to meet President McKinley and see if I couldn't get him to understand the plight of the working kid."

"Haven't you ever heard of the court of public opinion? That's how your strike got as much traction as it did two years ago—all those sympathetic articles and photographs really endeared you all to the masses." One eyebrow of hers jumped up and down.

Tommy grimaced. "We didn't win much for all our efforts."

Ellen rolled her eyes. "It got more than anyone expected a bunch of dirty, snot-nosed kids led by a fifteen-year-old boy with an eye patch to get. That was thanks to the boys' efforts *and* the reporting. Without reporters, no one gets to hear about anything that should or shouldn't be going on. If a tree falls in the forest, and the free press isn't around to take notes, no one's going to know if it made a sound."

When she put it that way, Tommy could see the appeal. Hadn't he spent a lifetime watching people get excited or dismayed merely by reading a few bold words on a page? And hadn't a headline been the very thing that spurred him to purchase a ticket to the Pan-American Exposition in the first place?

One by one, each of Tommy's problems presented themselves, and one by one, each could be solved by taking up a job like the one Ellen was trying to sell to him. The steady income would mean he wouldn't be going hungry or sleeping outside any longer. He could write about working children and all sorts of other issues that plagued him when he couldn't sleep at night, and he could have a whole column full of words to reel them in and convince them of the point instead of hoping they paid attention when you talked.

And then there was Linda. He could stay in town and make his case for being together, and he'd have something real and tangible to offer her besides an escape from being under the thumb of her parents. Even if her heart couldn't be won, he could still set her up at the lodging house, and she could be as free as he was.

Or maybe he could offer her something more.

Tommy cleared his throat. "You know, all that does sound real lovely, and I think I'd like to join the ranks. But I have this problem—"

"Name it," Ellen said. "Your talent is a rare find. If I can get my bosses to make a change for you, I will."

He tried not to smile while he spoke. "My gal works for the *Express* as a typist, and I'm not sure if working for different papers would be the best idea. She's a better storyteller than I am, or so everyone says. Would you have anything for her that might pay a little more? A reporting job, if I may be so bold?"

Ellen was quiet for a while, then popped her hands on her hips. "You know, you drive a hard bargain, Mr. Reid. Another gift from your background, no doubt. And I've already shown my hand like a nincompoop, haven't I?" She laughed. "You're very, *very* lucky I just lost my secretary to wifehood, or I would tell you where to stick your talent right now. I'll take your gal on, and if she's as good as you say at her storytelling, we'll see what happens. Does that sound fair to you?"

Fair? That sounded like the best deal in the world. Tommy bit the inside of his cheek to keep his emotions from showing. He couldn't stop the energy from flowing to somewhere though, and his fingers wiggled at his side. "That sounds fair. And that's nice of you to offer, thank you. She'll be thrilled."

"Indeed." Ellen closed her notepad and stuck her pencil behind her ear. "I've got to get all this to a typewriter, but you have my card. I expect to hear from you."

"Trust me, you will. You can count on that!"

Ellen shook her head as she turned away, but Tommy caught sight of a smile. Meanwhile, his own grin was wide enough to tear his cheeks. He knew getting a ticket to the Pan was lucky, but he would've never imagined it would end up like this—a real opportunity to make a difference for the newsies, Linda, himself, and who knew who else?

Now all he had to do was find Linda. He set out for her, a

whistle on his lips and the image of a cozy, furnished apartment with a full icebox on his mind.

CHAPTER TWELVE

Linda had circled the Esplanade twice by the time the sky began to pinken. She collapsed onto a bench in front of the fountain at its center, fanning herself. Her blistered feet would've felt more comfortable if they were on fire, she thought. At least then they would match her sunburned face.

She'd tried to tell her mother what her plans were, but her father stopped her, and she understood from his meaningful glances that now was not the time. She dreaded the reveal, but she also knew that her mother would succumb to her father's wishes eventually. If a few hours of being called ungrateful and wicked were all that stood between her and her new life, Linda could tolerate that.

But what she couldn't stand was not finding Tommy. She had so much to share, but she was more concerned about what happened at the Temple of Music. If President McKinley was shot, Tommy's trip to the Pan had been all for naught. *He must be devastated.*

The tragedy had done a number on the Pan's attendance, and despite the Electric Tower and all the other buildings set to illuminate soon, there were shockingly few people around. Those who had stayed were still taken aback from the events of the day, and stayed quiet, so all seemed peaceful.

Except for one, she guessed. What kind of a buffoon could be cheery enough to whistle now?

But then—no. She recognized the tune. It was the song Nina was singing when she and Tommy caught the end of her show.

His derby hat came into view, and Linda's heart soared. With no regard at all for her manners, Linda screamed, "Tommy!"

The man turned around, and indeed, the man looking absolutely flabbergasted was her Tommy Rabbit. "Linda?"

Her sore feet forgotten, Linda jumped off of the bench and grabbed hold of her skirts as she ran to place herself in front of him. "Are you all right? Are you hurt or anything?"

Tommy's face was frozen in a smile. "I'm sorry, what?"

"I heard President McKinley was shot! Were you there for it? Did you get the chance to meet him before it happened?"

"Never mind that. I'm sorry for the nation's loss of McKinley, but something amazing came out of the whole mess." Tommy took her hands in each of his. "I have the best news. I found a new job for you! And a job for me. I got interviewed by this nice reporter—you'll love her, I know it—and she liked the way I talked, and now I'm going to be a reporter for the *Courier*. Imagine that! I'm going from selling the papers, to being in them, to writing them myself. And you'll be my new reporter friend's secretary there, which is a step up from typist, isn't it? That'll mean more money." He paused. "If you want the job, I mean. Why are you looking at me like that?"

If her face was doing something funny, it was out of her control at the moment. Linda's head swam with the new information. Tommy wasn't leaving Buffalo after all. Not only that, but he'd also found security for himself and for her. It was the perfect situation. She couldn't have designed the plan better herself.

All her joy surrounding his machinations demanded to be felt all at once, and Linda started giggling, then shrieking with laughter. The confusion on Tommy's face only served to spur her on, getting louder and louder. Every eye on the Pan's grounds could be on her losing her mind, and she wouldn't have cared a bit.

Once the fits of laughter became shorter and more sporadic, Tommy said, "Linda, did I do something wrong? Is it so ridiculous to you?"

"No, no, you did fine," Linda said, finally catching her breath. "It's wonderful news, except I just told my family I was through with them, so all that extra money isn't going to do them any good."

"You did what?! But you love your family."

"I do love my family, Tommy, and I always will, but I've played Cinderella to them for too long." She beamed. "I'm going to live my own life now, like you do."

Linda nearly yelped from how tightly her hands were being squeezed. Tommy's weight shifted from foot to foot, and she watched his mouth half-form words without a sound.

"Well, what is it?"

"I—I have an urge to ask you something. A question. A question that just wants to pop right out of me. I want to pop a question."

"Tommy!"

This only generated more nervous energy. "Well, listen, okay? I'd like to tell you that marrying you—someone who I was sure hated me—"

"I never hated you. I just liked you, and that was terrifying."

"Linda, I beg of you, don't make this easier on me." Tommy's thumbs ran a thousand hurried circles over the backs of her hands. "I'd like to tell you that marrying you is a horrible idea, that we have our whole lives ahead of us, that we hardly know each other, and that I have any desire whatsoever to leave your side. But I can't tell you any of that because it's just not true."

Linda laughed again, and when Tommy's eyes widened as though scared she might start up another long fit, she only laughed harder.

"I know you have a past you haven't shared with me yet, and vice-versa. I know there's lots of things we don't know about each other. And I know your parents did something similar to this—"

"No, they didn't! They learned I was on the way, and then they got married whether they wanted to or not. This is the opposite, the very opposite. The truth is I can't think of a single reason why I wouldn't marry you." She squeezed his hands back. "Well, I *can*, but those reasons don't sound scary. They sound like problems we can solve together."

"Well, of course nothing would sound scary to you. You nearly kebabbed a man today."

"Stop making me laugh this minute!" Linda said through giggles, trying her best to force a serious look. "But you know, I was reflecting on that a little while ago. I think I'm braver than I look."

Tommy kissed the top of Linda's head, and a feeling like she was glowing from the inside out washed over her. "Great minds think alike."

"What am I thinking right now, then?"

"I would never pretend I can read your mind, but if I tell you that I am inches from the most beautiful girl in the world, would you be able to read my mind?"

The smile fell from Linda's face as she broke down the meaning of his words. "Earlier today, when you said that about me being the most beautiful girl in the world to that creep, did you—you really meant that?"

Positively effervescent, Tommy laughed and brought his arms behind him—their hands still connected—and pulled Linda into a kiss—warm, soft, sweet, and charged with emotion. It was Linda's first kiss, and it was the best thing in the entire world.

When they broke apart, as if to congratulate them, all the buildings in the Esplanade lit up with electric light, and music played over the loudspeaker. A glow seemed to settle over the city, and she was at the heart of it all. Even the man-made ponds and lakes dotting the grounds winked at her with rippling reflections of the radiance around her. It all dazzled Linda, who decided that never in her life had she felt so happy. She looked back at Tommy, who'd never taken his eyes off her in the first place, and leaned against him, sighing with contentment.

"I like this," he said, pressing his hand to her cheek. "Now I can see you better."

She took her hand and placed it on top of his to keep it there. "You're too much."

That seemed to put an idea into Tommy's head. "Do you have a place to stay tonight? I think I have enough pocket change to rent a second room at the lodging house, provided they have room."

Linda pouted. "I promised my family I'd be back tonight, but I never said anything about tomorrow night. And you know, I wouldn't mind so much if they didn't have a spare room." Linda lifted herself on tiptoe to kiss his cheek. She hardly believed her own ears. Sharing a room! Who was this dauntless woman, and could she stick around a while longer? "You can always sleep on the floor."

Tommy laughed and pecked her forehead back. "You've got a deal."

YOUR READER TREATS

Thank you for reading *In Buffalo With You*. I sincerely hope you enjoyed it! Please consider leaving your honest review on Amazon or Goodreads. I'd love to know what you thought of my story!

This book's associated freebies—what I call reader treats—include a word search, fun facts, a crossword puzzle revealing the settings of my next five books, and an exclusive epilogue starring Aggie McCoy! For access, all you have to do is sign up for my newsletter! Scan the QR code below with your smartphone to get started, or go to https://fuentespens.ink/subscribe. After, turn the page to begin reading my next book, *In Charleston With You*.

IN CHARLESTON WITH YOU: CHAPTER ONE

Jacob

Jacob blew air into his gloved hands as he trudged through the snowy streets towards the fourth pub of the night. London's unforgiving December chill had all but numbed his hands now, but he could still feel the cold through his clothes, and it was getting painful to move.

I hope he's in there. I hope he's all right. And if he is, I'll kill him.

Pushing open the door to The Gardeners Arms, Jacob marched to the back of the room, past half-asleep men nursing their whisky, absinthe, or gin. With both hands on the stained oak counter, he called to the barman. "Is there a game still on in your back room?"

The barman looked up from the glass he was cleaning to give Jacob a quizzical look over the top of his bifocals. From experience, Jacob knew all the stations at which the barman's train of thought stopped while looking him over. First, Jacob would look eerily familiar to him. He'd think it was strange that a man—albeit with a completely different disposition—was walking into his pub for the second time in a night. Then the barman might notice the different clothes or the few shades of difference in their whiskey-colored hair, and it would dawn on him.

Predictably, this barman said, "Would you happen to have—"

"An absolute fool of a brother? Yes. Tobias Cartwright. Is he still here?"

The barman nodded and jerked his head in the direction of a door to the back room. Jacob nodded his thanks and braced himself for whatever he was about to find.

The tang of sour, cheap beer assaulted his nostrils as he pushed the door open, followed quickly by something exceedingly more pungent and sickeningly familiar. A round, water-stained table littered with playing cards stood in the center of the room surrounded by mismatched wooden chairs. Half a dozen men in various states of sobriety stood not near their poker game, but huddled around something off to the side. Or someone.

"He doesn't look so good."

"'Ow many 'as 'e 'ad?"

"Not more than three pints."

"Three? My nan drinks three at suppertime."

Jacob's stomach sank like a stone. Sure enough, when he approached, a scarfless, coatless Tobias lay crumpled in a heap on the floor.

One bystander looked up to catch a glimpse of Jacob's face, recognized the family resemblance, and stepped aside to let him through. Jacob dropped to the floor to assess the night's damages. A quick pat on his thigh confirmed Tobias had lost his wallet and whatever was inside. That off-putting stench that first hit Jacob had indeed been Tobias's vomit, which formed a chunky puddle beside his pale, grimacing face. He was drenched in sweat and moaning, but thank God, he was still breathing.

Seeing his little brother in excruciating pain made Jacob heartsick. Tobias was more of a victim than anything else. They'd be long gone by now, but the prats Tobias ran with knew exactly how much fun he'd provide them—at his own expense—if only they could lure him to a card game. One lager would be all it took to begin his unraveling—which made him easy prey.

Tobias coughed, and he strained to whisper, "Is that you, Jacob?"

"It's me."

"I'm sorry," Tobias croaked. "I-I just couldn't stay away."

The brotherly love evaporated. What Tobias said was true, but that didn't stop it from feeling like a lazy excuse. Jacob ground his teeth together to keep from snapping, *Yes, you could have! If you would ignore your dodgy friends and take up a job like I've begged you, we wouldn't be in this mess!* It was a declaration not unlike several he'd strung together in his head over the past handful of years since their mother—with her saintly patience and soothing voice—succumbed to illness. Lately, they sat on his tongue with greater and greater weight.

But losing his patience with Tobias wouldn't be productive now, would it?

Jacob lightly smacked each of Tobias's cheeks. "Come on, now. You've had your fun, haven't you? It's time to go home."

"Mmph," was all Tobias could manage.

Realizing the show was over, the onlookers disbanded. Jacob talked one of them into fetching something to force Tobias back to this side of sobriety while he dragged Tobias up off the ground by the underarms. The man returned with a pint glass packed full of snow.

Again, Tobias moaned. "What am I meant to do with that?"

"You open your mouth, and down the hatch it goes," Jacob said, nodding his thanks at the man as he took the glass from him.

The man shrugged. "I would've suggested we stuff it somewhere else. Down his jumper, or down his—"

"You're mad!" Tobias screeched. As he did so, Jacob took hold of his jaw and tilted the glass forward until a gob of snow slammed into Tobias's open mouth. Tobias wrenched himself away from Jacob, shivering and spitting out snow. The other fellow barked out too hearty of a laugh for either of the Cartwright brothers' liking as he exited.

Jacob shrugged off his coat and threw it around Tobias's shoulders. At the same time, the jolt swallowing snow had given him wore off, and Tobias's eyelids drooped as he slouched into himself. In the nick of time, Jacob maneuvered himself under Tobias's arm to support his weight. Both of them were of an average size, and Tobias wasn't much heavier than Jacob, but the extra mass had Jacob's knees wobbling already, and it wasn't a short walk home.

"Jacob?"

"Yes?"

Tobias's voice was thick with tears. "Thank you."

Jacob groaned in relief as he took his first sluggish steps over the threshold. It wasn't much warmer inside his flat than on the frigid streets, but at least he was that much closer to his bed—the soft sheets, the pillows he'd just purchased the other day, the warm blankets he'd inherited from their parents...

All that and more on his bed, the only bed in the flat.

Jacob studied Tobias's lightless green eyes, untidy hair, and general disorderly appearance. The man was a wreck. No employer yet wanted to risk hiring someone with Tobias's tarnished reputation, which only made him feel worse, and that led him to pursue unseemly pastimes.

At least, that's what Jacob imagined was happening. They didn't discuss it much.

Whatever fueled Tobias's return to the cards and drink, he did always return, and those escapades always reached the ears of those who might've otherwise helped him. Jacob clinged to the hope that tonight wouldn't dramatically worsen the situation. The authorities weren't called. They shuffled away under the cover of night. Tomorrow was another opportunity for a help wanted sign to appear in some good-hearted soul's shop, or for an advertisement to be written just vaguely enough so as not to immediately disqualify Tobias.

Jacob was so caught up in this fantasy, he hadn't noticed Tobias slipped out of his grasp and stumbled into the bedroom—not until the first eardrum-shattering snore.

"Oh, no, you don't!" Jacob shouted as he dashed to reclaim what was rightfully his.

But it was too late. Clutching the duvet to his chest and out cold, Tobias would be unwakeable and unmoveable.

Smothered frustrations threatened to reignite in the pit of Jacob's stomach. This was supposed to be *his* bed. That was the deal when he agreed to house and clothe and feed Tobias until he had the means to live on his own. True, he let Tobias sleep there when he had an early morning job interview, but that was it, and that wasn't the case tonight.

He *deserved* all forty of the winks Tobias would get on the bed. Not every man in his twenties would put in so much time and effort in supporting someone who wasn't his wife, never mind venture into the freezing night to find a clod whose remorse would fade along with the alcohol's effects come morning.

If he vomits in my bed, I'll never forgive him.

As Jacob turned to go make up the couch for himself, Tobias murmured something in his sleep. Jacob only caught one word: "burden."

His response came as a reflex. "You're not a burden, Toby."

"I'll work it all out," Tobias said around another snore. "You'll see."

Jacob told him he was happy to hear it and exited, closing the door to the bedroom, hardly processing what his brother was going on about. He yawned. If he were more awake, his curiosity might have been piqued. But the sun would be rising soon, and Jacob preferred to rise with it. He retrieved both spare blankets from the linen closet, toed off his shoes, and collapsed onto the sofa.

Now, Jacob hadn't used the sofa in a long while. He wasn't home enough to engage in much lounging, and even when he was, the sofa was so associated with Tobias's sleeping space in

Jacob's mind that he avoided the area altogether, preferring to read or solve jigsaw puzzles at the dining table. But the discomfort he felt now was new, and the soft crunching sound when he shifted made him all the more perplexed.

A quick brush of his hand along each cushion yielded the culprit: there was something—many paper somethings, by the feel of it—in the cushion. Jacob groped around until he found a tear in the fabrics. A *deliberate* tear.

What have you been up to, Toby?

The answer was writing letters. Dozens upon dozens of letters were squirreled away in the cushions over the past several months, if the dates on the letters were anything to go by. When he was sure he'd retrieved them all, Jacob lit a candle and got to reading.

He meant to merely skim a few of them, just to be sure nothing scandalous or illegal was going on. At worst, Jacob imagined that Tobias might be sending love letters to a handful of women whom he believed might give him the time of day. The earliest letters indicated that was exactly what Tobias had in mind. Odd that he would choose to have the ladies address him by the brothers' shared middle name, Joseph, instead of Tobias, but maybe the anonymity was part of his fun.

Then, about three months into this epistolary hobby, the number of ladies to whom he was writing dropped in number until only one remained—a woman named Vivi. She wrote with the graceful penmanship, fine paper, and high-quality ink of someone from far more wealth than Jacob generated as a stenographer. Her letters had a delicate floral perfume applied, which Jacob appreciated. Even an untrained nose would've been able to identify the rose and orange blossom in the scents. He recalled their respective meanings without needing to reference the books he inherited from his mother—*love*, and *your purity equals your loveliness*.

Jacob smiled. An orange blossom was one of the dried flowers his father pressed between the pages of a certain lady's books purchased from his shop. That lady would become his wife, and Jacob and Tobias's mother. Both brothers inherited their father's green eyes and fleshy nose, their mother's bronze skin and airy laugh, and a mutual love of floriography.

But there was no way an American girl could know about the Victorian language of flowers that brought his parents together. Americans didn't know or care about such things, did they?

Nevertheless, Jacob was intrigued, and that was a good thing. It was only this piqued curiosity that led him to discover the real reason Tobias was using his middle name in their correspondence—and likely the reason he began writing Vivi in the first place.

Incensed, Jacob burst into the bedroom just as the sun's rays decided to do the same. "You're engaged!"

Tobias didn't stir. In one fluid motion, Jacob ripped off the covers. Tobias's legs shot up to his chest. Shaking violently, Tobias used one hand to search for a source of warmth. When he found none and realized what happened, he blearily regarded Jacob. "What are you on about?"

"You're *engaged*," Jacob repeated, paying no mind to how his increase in volume caused Tobias to wince. "And you used my poetry to woo her!"

"Can we talk about this in a few hours?"

"We absolutely cannot. You need to sit up, pick up a pen, and write to this girl that you can't possibly marry her."

Tobias wilted. "I can't."

"What are you talking about? Of course—" Jacob's eyes widened. "No, you can't, can you? You'd be breaking her heart, and you don't want to do that. You don't want to be cruel."

Tobias sighed. "There's more to it than that. You don't understand. But if you make me a strong cup of something piping hot and swear on your life to leave me be until evening afterward, I'll explain myself as well as I can."

IN CHARLESTON WITH YOU: CHAPTER TWO

Genevieve

Bathed in moonlight and sprinkled with topsoil, Genevieve prepared to immerse herself in the most recent arrival from her darling Joseph.

It'd been so long without one of his letters to keep her mind occupied while she tended to the gardens. After she woke up half the household singing to herself while sowing alyssum seeds a few weeks ago, her father begged her to keep her hobbies to the daylight hours. Much the same way that he must have asked her mother to do the same many years ago.

Neither Genevieve nor her mother could oblige him, of course. Their bodies prefered the midnight hours over any other.

Now she had new reading material to keep her heart and mind warm, even as January did its best to chill her to the bone. On nights like these, she was glad to let down her long, rose-red hair to keep the back of her neck protected. She tucked a lock behind her ear as she studied the foreign stamps and careful handwriting, imagining how Joseph might pronounce her full name in his accent.

With one fluid movement of her women's shears, the envelope split open to reveal a single piece of paper. Genevieve pouted. No poems or other additions this time. He didn't always include them, and Joseph always wrote less than she'd like, but to send such a short response after she poured her heart in her last letter? She found that odd. And troubling.

She slipped out the paper.

> Dearest Vivi,
>   As ever, receiving mail from you is my greatest joy, and nothing has meant more to me than knowing you share these sentiments.

Genevieve beamed. This was Joseph's poetic side shining through.

> So please understand that every word I've penned in this letter was chosen with the utmost care and respect for you. I think only of preserving your happiness.

That was the word that gave her pause—*preserving*. As if he knew of a threat against it. Genevieve bit down on her bottom lip and pressed on.

> I confess that the romance of it all swept me away, and I've expressed feelings for you that, upon reflection, are not as strong as I believe they would need to be to support a marriage. This revelation was devastating for me, but not half so much as learning a decade from now that we only contribute grief to each other's lives.
>   I want only the best for you, and I simply cannot accept that I fall into that category. Please do not attempt to convince me otherwise, but please do write back if you find the time. I value the friendship we've kindled, and I don't wish to lose it, thought I'd understand too if you never wrote me again.
>   This will be the last you hear from me if I don't hear back from you.
>   All my affection,

Joseph

Genevieve dropped the letter, lest she give in to the urge to reread it until the words lost meaning. She wasn't angry—though she imagined that might come later—but mystified. Desperate for something solid to cling to, Genevieve sank her fingers into the earth and took deep, cleansing breaths until the lightheadedness subsided.

They had plans. They were imperfect, half-formed plans that would've sounded mad to a normal person's ear, but they were plans nonetheless. He was supposed to board a shop the moment he'd saved up a reasonable amount of money, then they'd get married and start a new business, a new life—one that had absolutely nothing to do with Hathaway Fine Chocolates.

She looked to the full moon, as if the answers could be found in its faraway craters if she looked long and hard. Genevieve felt her mother's presence during these nocturnal outings. Both women had more in common with wildflowers than the delicate blooms they loved to care for. But unlike her mother, Genevieve wasn't encouraged to flourish in her own way.

That was what Joseph promised her: the chance to put down roots elsewhere. In fact, that was what Joseph purported to want for himself. So why send her a thing like this?

Maybe it has to do with me after all.

But no, that didn't ring true. She couldn't put her finger on why, but it felt like there must be another explanation. Joseph was capable of great eloquence in his poetry as well as astonishing bluntness, but he used his poetic pen to break her heart. Why, unless he cared?

"So what's the issue, Momma?" Genevieve asked the moon, leaning back on her palms. "If not me, then what? Fear? Financial worries? His brother posing a problem?"

All of her guesses made for reasons that were difficult to swallow. She tried to let her worries go and turned her attention back to the tasks at hand, but the seeds of a new scheme were already sown. If she could eliminate whatever risk preoccupied Joseph, perhaps she could convince him to give her a chance. She felt in her bones that they could be happy together. Certainly, they'd be a better pair than any of the gentleman callers that knocked on her door in recent years.

But there was only one thing that could eliminate such enormous risks as coming to another country to meet with a practical stranger, and that was capital.

As she moved from caring for the flowers to the herbs and vegetables, Genevieve warred with herself. In some ways, it would be the easiest thing in the world to ask her father for help. Just open the mouth and ask the question—those were the only steps.

That, and tell her father Joseph existed in the first place. She'd been putting it off for so long, and now she was kicking herself for it.

Her heart raced as she gathered her gardening tools and approached Hathaway House's carved oak doors. The Victorian-style mansion's color looked tantalizingly close to melted butter as the sun began its ascent, and Genevieve was tempted to sneak into the kitchen, steal a slice of bread and butter, and head straight to bed.

A servant took her shawl, gloves, and basket of tools away, and who did she find awake in the study but her father, listening to "A Bird in a Gilded Cage" at a low volume, hardly touching the plate full of chocolate squares on the end table next to his wingback chair.

"Daddy, what are you doing up?"

"*You* woke me up, dear girl," he replied with a drowsy, teasing smile under his bushy auburn beard, "when you snuck out. Though you make a poor rogue. You don't stray from the grounds, you're always caught in the act, and instead of coming home smelling of men's cologne or alcohol, you come home smelling like magnolias and camellias."

Genevieve chuckled along with him while guilt made pudding

of her insides. One can't come home smelling like a man when the object of one's affections is an ocean away, but he wouldn't have known to take that into consideration. Sure, she'd made no secret of the fact that she'd stumbled upon a few friends to write, but she never disclosed her growing fondness for Joseph. It surprised even her. One night she was writing about her most secret desire to open a flower shop of her own, and the next thing she knew, they were planning a marriage and exchanging secrets like children planning to run away, all the way across the street.

Her father handed her a sweet chocolate from the dish—heart-shaped, with purple flecks from the violet petals mixed in—as he went on. "But you're in earlier than I thought you'd be. Normally I don't hear the door open until well past dawn. Is something the matter?"

This was it. She had to speak now, before she lost her nerve. "I have a strange request for you."

His eyebrows lifted.

"Well, first a confession, then the request." Genevieve dug her nails into her palms, using the pain to propel her through the next few sentences. She took a deep breath. "Among the friends to whom I've written is a man I've actually—well, I'm in love with him."

Her father slowly, painfully turned to stone in front of her eyes. Not a hair or muscle moved. She could practically hear her declaration echo. There was no footfall from the servants, either. She'd stopped time in Hathaway House. Perhaps even stopped his heart.

No, not stopped. She recognized the heaviness of the quiet. She'd broken her poor father's heart. She'd broken *them*, the uneasy peace and understanding that first settled over them when her mother died and never lifted. The shards of it laid at her feet like broken glass, and she didn't know how either of them could carry on.

Her father's voice was reduced to a whisper. "I have so many questions."

"And I'll answer any of them. All of them. It's Sunday, isn't it? We—no, *I'll* cancel any engagements we might have, and I will spend the entire day answering your questions and—"

He held up a hand for silence and closed his eyes. "Just tell me what your request is."

But how could she now? How could she put another dagger through him? Tears pooled in the corners of her eyes. She expected anger and shouting, and she'd prepared herself for it, but to watch this happen to him—to witness him feeling powerless and inconsolable—was far worse than any punishment or insult he could've hurled at her. "I'm so sorry."

"No," he said, his voice firm. "Tell me, Genevieve."

She nodded and looked up at the chandelier to keep the tears from falling. "He—Joseph, er, Mr. Cartwright—expressed concerns about us being together. He thought we would make each other miserable, but I don't think so. I wanted to ask if you would be willing to fund his trip to America, so we could see if we were truly compatible."

Again, her father's lack of answer produced a deafening quiet that could scarcely be heard over the roar of her heartbeat in her ears. If he said no, there would be little else she could do to raise funds. Being a wealthy man's daughter, acquiring a job—even as a secretary for her own father—would shock and scandalize the wing of Charleston society the Hathaways fraternized with regularly. *Hathaway Fine Chocolates isn't doing that poorly,* they'd whisper, *is it?* Then there'd be more gossip, rumors would pop up like weeds, and then where would her father be?

Hurtling towards bankruptcy, to be sure.

At last, her father spoke. "But why would you tell me?"

Genevieve frowned. "What do you mean?"

"You could have boarded a ship to go see him, instead of the other way 'round, and concocted a story to convince me to fund it. You could have gotten a job without my knowing, stolen what you needed, or done a hundred other things that would've gotten you the money. But you chose to come to me for assistance—which I know you abhor—and to be honest. Why?"

Now tears were gathering in his eyes as well, which made Genevieve all the more emotional. When her other pen pals—the ones who were friends in the flesh before getting married or moving away—asked her why she never told her father about Joseph, she wasn't able to say. It wasn't childish anxieties over getting in trouble, or what people would think about their relationship. It was something deeper than that, and upon hearing the right person ask for an explanation to her behavior, the answer materialized on the tip of her tongue. She eked out in a cracking voice, "Well, I didn't want to hurt you. I'm sorry I kept you in the dark for so long, but I didn't know how to tell you. There are so many things I don't know how to tell you."

Her father beckoned her forward, took her head in his hands, and kissed her forehead. The gesture transported Genevieve to the night she learned her mother passed away. Both of them were crying in earnest now, especially Genevieve, who could hardly reconcile wanting her freedom with her desire to prevent loneliness from eating her father alive.

He sighed. "I'll fund the trip."

Genevieve took a step back to read her father's face, certain she misheard him. "You will?"

"I have conditions, of course. *Many* conditions. And you can bet that I'll be keeping a close eye," he said. "But we'll talk more after we rest. For now, let's finish this plate of chocolates."

They did exactly that, and Genevieve went to bed more at peace than she'd felt in years.

I hope you enjoyed this free sample of *In Charleston With You*.
You can buy the book at Amazon now!

About the Author

When she's not visiting what her mother calls "la-la land," Megan lives in Orlando with her boyfriend, a kitten rescued from a dumpster, and a lot of books she swears she'll read when she "gets a minute," whatever that means. Her favorite things in the world include iced coffee, office supplies, and telling you about those things. And writing, too. And lists!

Her website is https://fuentespens.ink. She's also found on Instagram and Twitter under the username @fuentespens. You can follow her on Amazon, Booksprout, and Goodreads, but to *really* stay up to date about book releases, the best thing you can do is subscribe to her weekly newsletter.

Scan the QR code below with your smartphone to go to her website and find all the links!

Made in the USA
Columbia, SC
20 August 2021